Kim Handley had her first stint in the working world at 16 working at an office and did not like it one bit. She soon realised that her life would be full of depression if she settled down and chose the 'Groundhog Day' life living as a robot in the social norms.

She took off at 17 to travel the world, became a dancer, studied another language and at 31 she finally admitted defeat and reluctantly settled down in a job and started living in the rat race. Here is where she found the true excruciating pain of boredom and so started to seek escapism by writing. She wanted to write a book whilst she was going through a journey, in order to express her angry emotions and so created a fictional book based on true events.

Kim Handley

THE MESSER

AUSTIN MACAULEY PUBLISHERS™
LONDON • CAMBRIDGE • NEW YORK • SHARJAH

Copyright © Kim Handley 2024

The right of Kim Handley to be identified as author of this work has been asserted by the author in accordance with sections 77 and 78 of the Copyright, Designs and Patents Act 1988.

All rights reserved. No part of this publication may be reproduced, stored in a retrieval system, or transmitted in any form or by any means, electronic, mechanical, photocopying, recording, or otherwise, without the prior permission of the publishers.

Any person who commits any unauthorised act in relation to this publication may be liable to criminal prosecution and civil claims for damages.

This is a work of fiction. Names, characters, businesses, places, events, locales, and incidents are either the products of the author's imagination or used in a fictitious manner. Any resemblance to actual persons, living or dead, or actual events is purely coincidental.

A CIP catalogue record for this title is available from the British Library.

ISBN 9781035847266 (Paperback)
ISBN 9781035847273 (ePub e-book)

www.austinmacauley.com

First Published 2024
Austin Macauley Publishers Ltd®
1 Canada Square
Canary Wharf
London
E14 5AA

I would like to thank all the people who are in my life, who have left my life and are yet to be in my life.

People that come into your life even for brief moments give you lessons. They both make and break you.

I would like to thank my friend Anne-Marie Leahy who has patiently listened to all of my crazy ideas, failings, and successes with a listening non-judgmental, supporting ear. In life you find your family, not through blood, but through soul connections and my Anny is certainly that.

A story of a woman who has emotionally recovered from a relationship with a heroin addict and falls in love, but she does not know if she is being manipulated, or if it is all in her mind. After a year of emotional turmoil, Kim finds out who she really is and discovers a darker side of her that she happily succumbs to.

The dust had settled from Kim's previous life. She had what she had prayed for in her darkest times, full of trauma, entrapment, and hopelessness. Peace. She had peace. She had obtained a stable, but boring, payroll job to pay the bills. Her home was always spotless and it always boosted a smell of essential oils and fresh washing.

She remembered her time living with her parents, who were both heavy smokers, the old school types who turned the heating to full blast with no windows open, which created a fog of smoke that circled around the room, trying to escape, before finally absorbing into the ceilings and walls, turning them yellow with each passing day. She would watch her mum fall asleep as the cigarette burned down until it was a bent fag of ash. She was sure that the term "Fag Ash Lil" had referred to her mother.

She had adopted two black cats and was solely missing a dog due to work commitments. She lived near the fields around where she had grown up. It was a quiet cul de sac with neighbours that were mostly Karens and jobs worth, but overall ok. Her dream home would be a cottage or a farmhouse, away from every fucker else, surrounded by huge fields, and a river, and she would reside with a collection of rescue dogs, cats, foxes, chickens; whatever animal wanted to come and live with her it could.

Fortunately, or unfortunately (you decide), the opportunity for Kim to find a good man and be a stay-at-home animal mum had never arisen. She was seething and resentful that she had to work and look after herself. From an early age, she had always relied upon herself, but boy, she really despised working. In her ideal life, she dreamt of days in nature, walking the dogs, practising yoga, going to the gym and steam room, reading, cooking, and feeling whole.

She did wonder about being married, as she was a very nurturing person and always daydreamed of a rugged, hard-working man. The thought of him coming home from work and her having dinner ready and a bath run for him. She enjoyed the idea of this nurturing role very much but had never picked the right man who could look after her. Kim often wondered why this ideal of hers had been outdated and why on earth women wanted to work all day and be slaves to such a soulless system.

Was it because back in the day when women did not work, they were in a way slaves to men? If you got stuck with a bad man, it would have been a godawful life. So yes, here Kim was like so many other millennials, not having anybody to rely on, living alone, no savings, living pay cheque to pay cheque, and battling their overdraft each month.

Who would not want to be looked after? she pondered, as she turned on her PC full of anxiety, barely being able to breathe as she opened the day's e-mails to complete another day in her payroll job. The queries started to flood in, one after the other, ping, ping, ping. Each query was something new that she had no clue on how to resolve, and so the battle began of the exhausting mission to learn how to do something, with no way of knowing how whilst being under time restraints as employees needed to be paid on time and correctly.

The job had been like this since day one around a year and a half ago. She kept sticking it out in the hope that it would get easier, but the longer she stuck around, the more problems came from out of the woodwork. She was having sleepless nights from the stress; her anxiety was bad and she was waking up in panic at 3am. She resented so much that a shitty job (she thought all jobs were shitty) was taking over her happiness and her soul was dying each day.

She had worked as a carer previously for people with learning disabilities and although she absolutely loved the cleaning, cooking and caring, she could not deal with the shift patterns anymore. She never had a sleepless night in that job though. She was never stressed and she loved the physical aspect of running around burning calories all day and looking after people. But now her current job was a mental stress, learning payroll calculations and it was such an intellectual bore off for her.

It was Bank Holiday in May. Kim had been dabbling on a dating website that afternoon. She had not been with anybody since she finally freed herself from her heroin addict, junkie ex-boyfriend. She had worked on herself for just under a year, and other than work, her personal life and well-being were in peak condition. As she was scrolling, she thought to herself, God, I cannot even be arsed to even go on a date.

It seemed like an effort for Kim to even put mascara on these days and the thought of a man ever entering her home again suddenly filled her with dread. Kim figured at that moment that she could not be bothered with dating; she had given her heart and soul to Lee (her past love) and she felt at that time she may not have the balls to love somebody again. She did secretly want somebody to just swoop in and be her king, take her away from working and sweep her off her feet and away from all the stress.

There were, in fact, many men who were willing and had offered this to her. But unfortunately, Kim was wired wrong; just like so many other silly women like her, she liked the bad boys. What she wanted from a man did not seem to exist. A man full of confidence, testosterone, free, a leader but also loyal and kind, out to find his queen. Unfortunately, these attractive males, full of testosterone, brash and with soaring confidence, were usually heading straight to prison.

They were not loyal, were nearly all on the psychopath spectrum, and were inherently involved with one or all of the AAAs (abuse, addiction, and adultery).

As she sat scrolling, a man caught her eye. He had a huge gold chain around his neck. Kim thought that it looked ridiculous but the mean frown and look on his face started to wake up her pussy. The next photo he had, was of him with a big spliff in his mouth. She absolutely cringed at herself. 'You are 37 years of age,' she told herself. 'You are looking for somebody to support you. Does this look like the type of guy you want?'

But yet again, only found this type of man attractive and had the option to dabble with the devil as she was independent and had nothing to lose but her self-respect and dignity. She continued looking at him.

'KIM!' The good voice in her head screamed at her.

'If you are going to go for this sort of man, you might as well have stuck with Lee.'

'No!' The bad voice said to Kim.

'Lee was a stealing, heroin addict. You are hardly going to fall for that again, are you? It is just a bit of flirting.'

'What is the point of switching from Brandy to Jack Daniels when you should be looking for a fruit smoothie?' Her good voice said to herself.

The voices faded and she was already automatically sending her number to him. One of her must have's is a deep voice. Previously in the dating world, she would spend time messaging somebody, and then when she finally spoke to them, their voice was unattractive. It all boiled down to Kim's authenticity. She was a cave woman at heart. She loved deep-voiced, big-built, and strong grafting type men.

She would not be seen dead looking at an office type or a modern male who pruned his eyebrows, etc. Fuck that. Her phone rang and it was him! She was a bit taken back by how quickly he had responded with a phone call. His confidence and his deep grimy voice came pouring through the speaker. 'Oi, listen yea, just thought I would give you a quick call to drop my number.' Then he put the phone down. His voice was so deep and husky, that it had her attracted to him immediately.

His accent was unusual. He was HMP material for sure. Why was she even going to entertain this, she didn't know. From his looks and further examination of his profile pictures (his slick hair styles and being sat in a trailer) and his accent, she had a feeling he was a traveller. She sent him a voice note and asked if he was a traveller. He immediately sent a video back of his trailer. Kim had always loved the thought of being a traveller woman.

Her perception of them was that the woman was to stay at home, look pretty, cook and clean, and keep a lovely home and the men would go and graft and give them money for shopping, etc. People tend to think of the Tinkers when you say, travellers. The ones who leave the rubbish everywhere and have no respect for the land they move through. But Kim was solely thinking of the lush static homes and the permanent sites that were now more popular within that community.

Kim shut herself down as she was being ridiculous. This is how she became—it wasn't the man really that she wanted, it was the rescue, the way out of work. But she could and would only do it for love. If she wasn't so deep, by now she would for sure be living securely like the thousands of other women who marry for stability and not love. Kim could not do that; it was so odd to her that people could be with people just for the benefit of security. She would be miserable.

Kim shut her fantasies down as she knew she was being ridiculous, but she also loved the butterflies in her stomach. She felt alive again. 5 years she had been with Lee. She was fiercely loyal and even if Tom Hardy had walked into the room, she would have only had eyes for her man. So now finding somebody attractive after 5 years with Lee was quite thrilling.

True to his word, he rang her, and once again his voice had Kim's stomach in knots. It was almost as if he was growling, rather than speaking. She had never heard anything quite so feral. The conversation was a bit weird. He had a northern twang and spoke with a few Irish words in between. Kim recognised the northern twang and asked him if he was from Yorkshire. He said he had been living in Leeds as he had been adopted into a family up there.

His real family were from Leicester and so he had been reunited with them some time back and now he resided in

Leicester. Kim told him she had once lived in Doncaster, and he laughed and said he had just left Marsh Gate that year. Kim knew that was a prison from researching Lee's life, trying to find out what category of prison Lee had been in and what he had been in prison for, but she never found out.

Lee had said it had been for fighting but Kim was sure that you didn't get a 5-year stint for a simple fight. Kim could not help but let out a laugh.

'Oh, so you are fresh out of HMP. Nice.'

He laughed, almost impressed that she knew what Marsh Gate was, and it seemed to set off a base attraction between them both. Kim knew what he was about immediately and he knew that she was a diamond in the rough sort of woman. Once again, he cut the conversation short and said that he had to go and raise some money. Kim cringed at the immaturity of that sentence—it was the sort of thing that she had said with her friends at 14, trying to get a raise together to smoke a draw on the bong, whilst her mum was at the bingo.

'What is your name?' Kim said.

'Mushy.' And with that, he slammed the phone down.

That evening, he sent her a video of him in his trailer. It was not the glamourous static home that she had imagined, and it was not on a traveller's site. It was a trailer dumped on an industrial site between a scrap yard business and a white van sales carpark. She studied the video and paused it to study the freeze frames. The bedside cabinets had a few burner phones on, huge bags of weed and grinders, wads of cash and a few watches.

The video spun around and proceeded outside where he had a pan of baked beans cooking away on a burner stove. WTF, she thought. She, at that moment, wanted so badly to block him, but then her compassionate side spewed in and she thought: The guy has just come out of prison, with no money, and no home.

She decided not to block him at that moment, as it would come across as shallow and materialistic, even though her new goal was to be materialistic by having a man's money to support her. The next man she wanted to look after her, she didn't want to work, she wanted to stay at home with her fur babies.

'Remember, Kim,' said a voice in her head.

'He's a homeless traveller, fresh out of prison, cooking baked beans on a burner stove; it's not on track to being a kept woman is it? Block him.'

Her phone pinged again—another topless video—this time she could see a huge tattoo on his chest of a pit bull. 'Jesus Christ, Kimberly,' she said to herself. His piercing blue eyes jumped out of the screen and he had the nicest lips and dimples, and his body was huge. She was mesmerised. She watched the video about 15 times just to hear his voice and see his eyes. She knew she was being ridiculous, but also loved this feeling, this excitement. It was such a welcome break in her boring, monotonous life.

Over the next few days, he sent her a few messages (nothing but crumbs really). He phoned her at night times but always the duration would last no more than a minute. It was very erratic. This time, though, he asked her when he could see her and arranged a Sunday. The arrangement was that Kim would make her way to his. Kim immediately went into boss mode as per usual.

'I'll go and pick him up, we will go to dinner, after dinner we will go for a long walk in the Peak District. Oh God no, that is too much for a first date, I will book us into the gym and we will go to the steam room, and then chill in the jacuzzi. I'll buy him a pass. Maybe afterwards, we can go for a coffee, but he doesn't seem like he is the sort of guy that is a coffee type.'

She became angry at herself.

'Why am I doing the planning again? I do not want to be in control. I want somebody else to be the boss for a change. I want somebody to try for me and plan a day for me. I don't want to be in control.'

Throughout the whole of her relationship with Lee, she was the boss and in control. She had to be, otherwise, she would have lost him to the drugs. That was her mindset at the time, if she kept everything smooth for Lee, then he would not go under, but the drugs were so powerful that no consequence was enough to stop him. She paid for the holidays to act as a detox for him, organised places to live for him, paid his rent when he was struggling, along with arranging and paid for all the dates, and always paid for meals.

It was she who arranged the well-being nights of massage, lit candles in the room, incense sticks on the burn, and gave him foot massages, and back massages. And in return, she was cheated on, robbed, lied to, manipulated, and punished. Her taking control was bringing up resentment and she regretted telling Mushy that she had made plans for them both on Sunday.

She wanted to drive down to Norfolk on the Sunday as it was boiling hot for the month of May and she wanted to make the most of life after the lockdown, but she had a feeling he would only want to meet her for an hour or so, so she was torn. 'Do I ask him and see if he's available to come to Norfolk or is that desperate?'

She hadn't heard from him for a day or so and Kim thought, Oh, here we fucking go. Here comes the testing; pulling back and seeing how she reacts to the ghosting test. She was almost relieved actually and ready to forget this dangerous, stupid path. She got on with her day but after deciding to forget him, her phone pinged. "Sorry, babe, I was out last night and lost my phone". Instantly, Kim was again put off.

What is a 35-year-old going out on a Wednesday and getting so that drunk, he loses his phone (This was her interpretation of it)? She hadn't got the facts that this had happened but that is what she had assumed. She found herself almost in a trance as she rang the number. He picked up and she jokingly asked him what on earth he had been doing that night to have lost his phone. He confirmed he had a drink and had probably left it around his cousin's house. They started chatting a little and Kim mentioned how beautiful his baby blue eyes were.

He said he was almost blind in one eye due to a fight with two scag heads who he'd seen shooting up in a kid's playground and so he approached them and started fighting with them. One of them pulled out a bottle and threw the contents (likely ammonia) in his face. Kim felt bad about his eye but Kim delighted in the mutual hate they both had for smack heads, crack heads, spice heads, the lot of them. It was only because of what Lee had put her through, anyone who knows a smack head, knows that they are all the same.

Robbing, dirty cunts, who have the human sucked out of them and become monsters and zombies. They didn't deserve to tell their individual stories on why they were the victims; in Kim's mind, the victims were the families, the unborn children, the children left to rot and starve at the hands of these possessed demons. They would do anything for the drugs, so she couldn't understand why they were always portrayed as the victims. She knew she would have more compassion if she hadn't experienced one.

She hoped that in prison, Mushy would have beaten a few up just for good measure. He mentioned he was into going to the gym every day, but since being in prison, he had gotten a bit chubby due to 23-hour lockdowns because of Covid. He said he'd got out of prison and had been in a bare-knuckle fight that he'd committed to before going to jail and when he'd had the fight, he'd felt sluggish. Kim got the impression he was lying—just call it instinct.

Kim again cringed at the immaturity. All these conversations of fighting, drugs, raising cash, drinking on a Wednesday—it was a far cry from travel, yoga, nature, and animals she was into, but here she was, ever aroused by the bad boy.

It had taken a good year to get her self-esteem back from what Lee had put her through. He had made her feel so worthless by cheating and lying that she had not even been able to look in a mirror at herself for very long. She would do her hair but never could look at her face for long. It was like she couldn't bear to even look herself in the eye. She had slowly found herself again and was comfortable in her own skin.

She wasn't the sexiest girl by a long way, but when she was at her best health-wise—sleeping well, cycling, eating the rainbow, drinking copious amounts of water, and visiting the steam room—her health glowed through her skin. Her eyes when she was with Lee were soulless, dead, and sad. But now that bright hazel vibrancy was back, in what she had thought her best asset. She had never been into makeup, she thought makeup was horrible. She likes a bit of mascara and eyebrows put on, but nowadays the contouring trend is out of control.

Makeup was shuffled on in the bucket load, and so she was feeling good that she knew she could be able to entice Mushy with her confidence and natural glow. She wanted to mesmerise him; she never seemed to have the upper hand. Men always think that it is only the nice guys who lose, and she wanted to add to this semi-true fact that the nice girls always lose as well!

It had been a few days and he hadn't texted or phoned. 'Round 3' Kim giggled as she got on with her own boring life. Kim had always failed the men's tests spoken about previously. As soon as she was tested, it was game over for her as she would lose her shit and text them abuse and say how furious she was that they were running games on her. Game playing was insulting, it fucked her head up mainly because she was such a logical person. She never understood why people made that mess.

In the dating world, if Kim didn't like somebody or something that made her cringe, she would just say straight that she wasn't interested, there is no connection or interest in moving forward. Dress sense had been a big factor for Kim losing interest very quickly—she liked casual, and she wasn't a good dresser herself, but she was not going to look past someone wearing a pair of crocs. Voice was a big thing as mentioned before; and smell.

She had once been with a man for 6 months who on paper was perfect for her, you couldn't have found a more perfect man—loving, kind, hard-working, manly, beautiful soul, she wouldn't have had to have worked. He moved her into his nice home; he didn't want kids; they travelled, but one of the reasons was his pheromones. They just didn't match hers. He didn't smell at all, but it was the wrong smell for her and the wrong timing to settle down for her aged 26.

Kim swore she hadn't evolved at all. She couldn't stand society; she hated the system and longed for freedom somehow. Maybe that's why she was attracted to the Mushy types—they aren't necessarily bad boys, maybe the words bad boy should be changed to wild, free, non-conformant, full of testosterone, and so in the caveman days, you would want a man like that. You'd want them to protect you and so they would have to have an element of monster in them and that would make them highly valuable men—and Kim still wanted these qualities.

She hated the way society was trying to feminise men. It made her sick. The ever-ongoing attack on the working-class man.

Kim went a good 4 days without succumbing to Mushy's ghosting. She usually now would delete his number so she couldn't at times of desperation send that godawful message to somebody who is not interested in you to say "hey, how are you?", but she still had his number and as the Saturday afternoon passed in her dad's garden with a few Guinness and Blacks in her system, she was feeling that her inhibition was lowering. She had cut a lot of people off in that year.

People that she used to drink with. She'd had enough of herself. Kim could not stop with just a few, she was so rigid and routine-orientated, and her job kept her stagnant and stuck in a boring life every day, so once she let go with other reckless people, it went from 0-60 within a matter of minutes for her.

That first sip of Jack Daniels and the tug of nicotine from a menthol roll-up was just an immediate release, her whole body let go and all the stress and tension just disappeared, but as the hours progressed, she would be ordering cocaine with her friends, which enabled her to easily drink another bottle of Jack Daniels and smoke another 50 roll-ups, and ending up somewhere far from home. By the time she knew it, it was 6am, light outside, and she was having to drive back from wherever she had landed off her tits and in for the worse come down of her life.

It all usually happened around payday and so she'd have spent all of her money and now she would have to pay for it not only financially but also the means of feeling suicidal and hating herself with a vengeance (until the next month when it would happen all over again). It had all started in lockdown. She had never been into cocaine, and she still wasn't. She loved alcohol more. Cocaine was just a means to go on drinking—but she hated it, people chatting shit and being all deep for hours.

She'd rather be laughing and being silly on a drunken high. But both were toxic to her and so she had become a hermit to all associates and found herself in the safety of her dad's garden on Saturday afternoons in the sun with a few Guinness and Blacks to take away the cravings and keep herself in check.

She was tipsy in the garden and found herself thinking about Mushy who she had now funnily re-named "Big Joe

Joyce", an Irish bare-knuckle boxer who was an old, crazy man now. Her inhibitions were loose and her fury at why he had ghosted her had started to kick in. She rang the number but there was no answer, which infuriated her even more. Tipsy, she typed the message "keep your breadcrumbs, you prick".

She immediately regretted losing the challenge and quickly deleted all traces of his number. She decided that she was wasting energy wishing that he had texted her or been interested in her. She knew really if he was hounding her or as interested in her as she was in him, she probably would have lost interest anyway, and she cringed knowing that he was thinking the same about her due to her being overly keen and that made her sick. Besides, he was not husband material.

She'd just be treading down the same disappointing path and she felt relieved at her decision to check herself. She could put her silly, immature lusty feelings to the side and get on with life.

It was Sunday and although she had only drunk a few Guinness and Blacks, and shots of her dad's moonshine, she felt rubbish. She frantically spring cleaned, put the washing on, went for a steam room swim and cycle, and drank tonnes of water to try and eradicate any trace of unhealth. She had become petrified of feeling the way she used to after binges and so any slight feeling of a hangover sent her into a frantic panic of trying to redeem herself.

Her phone rang and it was his number as she remembered the 407 at the end. 'What you on about you fucking div. I was texting your old number and had forgotten that you have a new number,' he said. Kim had changed her number a few days back but he had obviously not stored it. She called bullshit because if he wanted to get to know her, he would have messaged her on the dating site or had some sort of trace of her new number.

Anyway, it wasn't like Kim was not ecstatic that he had phoned and yet again his voice had sent her into a sexual trance. He asked what she was doing on the Monday and asked her if she wanted to go for food on the Monday at about 2pm. Kim suggested they go for food and then sunbathe after as it was a lush month of sun.

The day arrived and she was full of excitement. She felt like a teenager but what she was really feeling was free. It was nice to be doing something different and exciting. She hadn't entertained another man since Lee, so it would have been 5 years of Lee and a year on her own recovering. She waxed, did her hair, and nails, had a beautiful golden tan, and her teeth were sparkly white. She packed a bikini and put on a croquet-knitted backless bodysuit and matching knitted shorts.

She was resembling her old self and the looks she used to have, although now she was older, it was harder to carry off, but she still had a few years left in her. Kim's ideal of attractiveness wasn't in trend. She loved the tiny, skinny body idea and although Victoria's Secret's runway models' bodies were unattainable for her only being 5'2 inches in height, she was happy with her 80s aerobic, stick-like body and big hair.

She typed in his post code into the sat nav excitingly. It was a glorious day, so she put the roof down on her battered Renault Meganne Convertible and relished driving as the sun was beaming down on her in the country lanes on the way there. The small country roads winding and weaving were a breath of fresh air. She loved seeing new things and places.

She pulled up to an industrial estate, a car park full of vans and a timber yard and a scrap business.

She rang him and said to him that she had arrived. 'Go through the vans, walk down, and you'll see my trailer. My doors open, just go in and wait for me. I'm just on a job, I won't be long.'

WTF, Kim thought. 'Cheeky bastard,' she laughed to herself. She found the random trailer in amongst the businesses. She opened the door, went in and sat down. Her heart started to beat out of her chest but it was soon calmed with how quiet and tranquil everything was. There was a huge wad of cash on the side, drug bags ready and packed up to sell. Very trusting of him, Kim thought. She could just take off with this money now.

She heard footsteps and as he walked in, he said, 'Hello.' Kim was instantly pleased with his looks which were way beyond her expectations from his photos online. He had something about him in his videos and photos but in real life, he was even more attractive. It was a weird combination as his looks were very boyish and sweet—blonde hair, piercing blue eyes, dimples—but he was also so rough and rugged and manly.

His body was huge, he was above 6ft tall, and his demeanour was menacing, aggressive, and commanded attention.

He was on his phone and whoever he was speaking to, he said, 'Yo, I might have a job to do in an hour yeah.' Kim laughed inside as she knew this was a ticket out of the date if he didn't like her. He sat down and there was an immediate comfort between them. It was like two friends who had not seen each other for a long time and had picked up exactly where they left off.

Kim recognised that connections like this were very special to her, as it was rare that she ever met anybody in life and clicked immediately with them, and so when she did, it had been a bond for life. Kim had no filter. She spoke to strangers as she would speak to her closest friends. She had no decorum and was free with everyone. He was completely Alpha Male, also comfortable and didn't give a flying fuck about anything seemingly. She could tell they were pleased with each other.

He picked up his phone after 10 minutes and told the same guy on the phone before that he would do that job tomorrow. He grabbed Kim's hand and said, 'I'm starving, let's go eat.' She was pleased that she had passed his get out of jail free card.

She got in his car and there were bags of drugs and another wad of cash in the drinks cup holders. He started to drive, and it was absolutely petrifying. He was doing 90mph down the tiny country roads whilst rolling a spliff and steering the wheel with his wrists. He took his top off and strutted in the pub garden saying hello to all the elders in a respectful manor for their age group. They sat on the bench outside by the river and the physical touching was immediate. They couldn't stop holding hands and touching each other affectionately. It felt incredible, to feel his huge hard working rough man hands grab her tiny thighs and waist and he moved his hand and grabbed the back of her neck and pulled her in for a kiss. He tried to put his tongue in her mouth, and it was awkward as they both had completely different kissing styles. Kim shrieked with laughter, and he relished in the fact that he was making her laugh. It was such a raw attraction.

They got back in the car and headed towards the nearest council estate that he was dealing in, with Kim praying for her life in the passenger seat. He'd smoked one spliff after another and she was uneasy about his drug use. He said he had obtained an injury when he used to play rugby and had to be on tramadol since and he was honest and said he was not right in the head either and so the weed calmed his mind. Kim was shocked as this guy was a 100 mph. fidgety, hyper, and full of energy and so she was baffled that if he was like this on tramadol and weed what on earth was he like clean.

He continued speeding around the estate, street after street stopping the car in a jolt to speak to every person he recognised. He clearly loved people and she watched people's faces light up as he made the time of day for each of them, but upon seeing their faces light up, she felt a bit silly because she concluded that he had this effect on everyone and she then doubted the 'immediate' connection she thought that they had.

They got back to the trailer and Kim was tired. She lay on his bed and positioned her thick, long hair across the pillow and casually positioned her body in a sexy shape that wasn't so obvious as a pose but was normal enough to show her hips and bum sticking out. He stood over her and his phone rang. He answered it and started talking all his gangster shit, but as he was talking, he was staring straight into her eyes. It drove her wild. He carried on talking and lay down next to her on his back. Kim leaned towards him and started stroking his lips and his chest whilst admiring him. She gently started licking his lips and as they started to kiss, he would pull away to say "yes" or "no" to whoever was on the phone. He cut his friend short and said, 'listen I'll ring you back' He dropped his phone on the floor and firmly pulled her towards him for a passionate kiss. He had the same energy as her. It was strong, confident and they both enjoyed all the affection as well as a little bit of filth. Kim didn't do all that fake acting porno shit. She was in tune with herself and her needs and wants. She liked a mixture and was earthy and sensual. He seemed more fire energy, but still had that affection and loving side. He was dominant and was pulling her hair and putting his fingers in her mouth. It was not her intention to have sex with him today. She wasn't planning or not planning to get sexual. She didn't play them games or wait for 3 dates before a kiss, but she hadn't been with anybody but Lee for 6 years and if she wanted sex, she decided she would have it and decided to have it the moment he pulled her bodysuit to the side and gently but firmly put his finger inside of her. Upon feeling how tight her pussy was, he let out an almost growl and bit her top lip hard.

She loved how nice she knew her pussy would feel to him all freshly waxed, oiled up, and so tight that he had to push hard just to get his finger in. It felt incredible to be able to let go. All her mind, body and soul to let go. She had NEVER been able to let go of Lee. She knew he had been up to all manner of sick things to obtain his drugs. When she was with Lee, she was rigid and stiff, and often during sex, she would start crying into the pillow with emotional pain.

But here she was, free to give affection and free to receive it. The tension built up even more and he pulled her tiny frame underneath him with ease and put all his weight on her whilst still kissing her and slowly but firmly put his huge cock all the way in deep. He left his cock deep in her and gently pushed the hair from her face whilst biting her neck. He started to then move and Kim, at 37 years old, had never had this feeling before.

He was so confident and composed and, with a clump of her hair firmly in his hand, started to fuck her whilst looking directly into her eyes. She was absolutely gone. He had a mean frown on his face, and he said to her whilst looking straight into her wide eyes, 'This is mine now, you're not to be with anybody else, ok?' Kim laughed inside but absolutely adored the dominance.

They both collapsed in a heap and immediately started to mess around again. She was so free and childlike with him, and as she laughed at his boyish behaviours, she watched his face light up as he puffed his chest out and felt manly in front of her. He pulled her back down on the bed and asked her to stay the night, but Kim immediately thought there is no hot water or a toilet flush, what if she would need to go for a shit.

She told him that she had cats at home and would need to go back and feed them, and let them back in home. She told him next time she would. After 10 minutes more, he was on the phone and heading back out to do more shenanigans. Kim drove her car home feeling incredible. She wished so much that she could re-wind the day and do it all over again.

Kim got back to normal life, and he had sent her a few nice text messages and had arranged to see her on Tuesday when he was home from Leeds. It was a Saturday, her favourite day. She cycled into town to sit outside Costa with a Soya Mocha and the day was especially hot. She had some tobacco left that she had scrounged from her dad as she sometimes liked a nightly roll-up with a cup of tea. Perfect, she thought, sun, coffee, fag, and a bit of people-watching.

She felt especially good that week as she had been to step class, aerobics, swimming, and an abs class. The feel-good feeling of health quickly passed though as early morning faded and, in the sun, she could feel the familiar pull of alcohol. She didn't want to go to her dad's safe garden today and she had nearly enough cut everyone from her life to become a spiritual hermit.

She tried to remember the words of her peers such as Theo Von, Russel Brand, and Jordan Peterson on finding a way to get through the craving—you must find something better to feed the craving, something adventurous. Kim was sad that she couldn't find the strength in her most of the time just to have a couple of social drinks. It was always one drink leading to carnage until 6am and the older she was getting, it was even more of a horrendous site in the mirror the next day. "Ping", a message from her friend, Zak, arrived.

"Do you want to come and have dinner and drinks at my dad's? I am in his garden". And just like that, on auto-pilot, she was off on her bike very quickly in a huff of excitement. 'I will just stay until 8pm,' she said to herself. She was already dying inside from the angry voice that was trying to remind her about tomorrow, about the money she did not have, about how it would all end.

It was begging her to turn her phone off and go and cycle to the country park or do a new canal route she had not done before, but she pushed them down and arrived "sensibly", she thought, with a few tins of mojito cocktails and gin and tonics in hand. She thought these tins of cocktails were too weak to send her from 0-60 as it was not like they were Jack Daniels or Brandy, which is what her crazy days were down to. She sat on his grass, sun beaming down on her face, body completely relaxed.

As she took a drag of her roll-up and a swig of her tin, her body completely relaxed. She relished these moments—it felt like freedom. She quickly prepared steak, salad, garlic bread, and rice, all in the name of lining her stomach and not letting the alcohol get to her with immediate effect. An hour later, it had not worked, and Kim and Zack were on the way to a pub. She knew this was going to happen.

She spotted a few cocaine dealers dotted around the pub on her way in. Her stomach sunk with disappointment knowing what the afternoon to evening would now become. The pub was quite empty and as they entered the pub garden, Zack's family sat on a big table. Kim felt relieved at the normality and quickly sat next to Zack's dad, who she had now grown fond enough of to call him pops even though his name was "Monkey Hanger" as he was from the Northeast.

He was around the same age as her dad and in her merry way wanted more people to come and join them and make the atmosphere better. She phoned her dad and asked him if he and his girlfriend wanted to come and join them at the table—he asked who was with her and so she put him on speaker phone and said, 'Zack's family and you will know his dad, Monkey, as you'll have been about the estate together over the years.'

In a stern voice, he said, 'Monkey from Stocking Farm?'

'Yeah. That is the one,' she replied, hoping that they would know each other.

'The same Geordie that shagged my wife, your mother, tell him to fuck off.'

The whole table erupted with laughter and Zack's sister turned to face Kim, and whilst laughing, said, 'I always thought that you had the same eyes as us!' Monkey swore he couldn't remember and said it wasn't true, but nobody cared either way.

Kim spotted Zack sneaking to the bathroom with a guy, so it was obvious he was going to go for a line. She felt a wave of panic as she thought the family atmosphere would be a deterrent. She should just go now, she thought. Get away whilst she can but by the time she knew it. a shot of sambuca was in front of her and the sun was going in, and all the normal family folk had headed home probably for a nice night in with munchies and the TV after a hot bath.

The youngers piled in a car and on the way back to Zack's, the guy next to Kim pulled out a bag and she sniffed a line from his hand. In the garden, around the garden bench, the drunken fun had disappeared and the deep and serious drug cocaine conversationalists had appeared, chatting utter shit under a blanket of false confidence, smoking a hundred cigarettes an hour it felt like. It was 9pm and cold. Kim had consumed 2 lines of cocaine but that was enough for her to hate herself.

The cocaine had run out and everyone was chasing around on their phones desperate for more. Kim consciously watched everyone and it was a huge wave of a sober moment and the realisation that if more arrived, then that would be it. So she excused herself to the toilet but instead ran out of the back gate into her car and drove home. She was ecstatic that she had made it home and it was 21:30, and as she had only drunk light drinks and a sambuca, she would be ok the next day.

Kim was on annual leave for the next few days. Big Joe Joyce said that he would come to Norfolk with her for the day, but he had not been in contact again so off she fucked on her lonesome per usual. She loved road trips to the beach and actually, it was lovely on her own as she went at her own pace and did whatever the fuck she wanted at whatever time she wanted. It was freeing.

She had the roof down on the car as she sped down the A47, one long road for 2 hours until she reached Norfolk. She had felt so human again after a few days off from work and this trip on the way down to Norfolk, seeing different sites and scenery on the way, is what she lived for. Refreshment of the mind, body, and soul. She pondered repeatedly on the thought of not having to work. She could do things like this every day (if she were being looked after).

'Anyway,' she said to herself. 'I am on my annual leave, stop thinking about fucking work, will you.' She reached Wells Next to the Sea. Last time she had come here was during lockdown when people had been summoned to stay in their houses by the government, not her though, she was on the beach and there was nobody on it, and it was such a magical moment. She made her way through the semi-crowded areas and found a nice spot outside an unused beach hut.

She took a deep breath of the sea air and the peace astounded her. She could see the heat waving off the sea line making wiggly shapes and behind her, the trees were a dark, lush green and the sand was white and talc powder-like. It could have easily passed as a tropical place that day. The day passed all to quickly and before she knew it, she was driving back to Leicester with tears in her eyes that her little day of adventure was over.

She lived for that adventure. No matter how small the trip, it just kept her alive going to places and getting out there. She was a lap dancer 20 years back and at that time it was so easy to earn a grand in a few nights and hop off to Costa Rica for a month. 'At least all my dancing days money was spent on travel and adventures,' she reminisced. There were all sorts of dancers back in the day. The ones that saved the money and had brought the house, or houses, outright.

The materialistic ones who spent their money on Gucci and Chanel, and the simple ones like Kim who were just grateful not to be in a normal job and wanted to avoid adulthood and responsibilities forever.

She arrived home with a wonderful welcome from her two black cats, Sassy and Bear. She was never away from them too long and had taken them with her on holiday to Newquay and in the car sometimes to visit her mum. Big Joe Joyce had contacted her with a text message saying "X". She felt her anger bubble up to the surface and she became so hot and furious. She was due on her period anyway but this sort of fuckery drove her up the wall.

'Who ghosts people and plays games at our age, or any age at all as a matter of fact,' she seethed. 'No contact from him at all blanked my last text for days on end, ghosted me for Norfolk, and now just a stupid X in a message,' she thought. She could not cope with somebody erupting her emotions like this. The anger was not healthy for her.

She texted him back quickly, "Hi, do not text me anymore. It won't be the same now if we meet up again anyway because now, I know you are playing stupid games, and now I will have my back up and I don't want to be in the company of somebody who I can't be free with. Bye, Mushy".

He replied immediately. "Listen, I do like you, on my life, I just live a totally different life, it's just difficult". Kim pondered over the text. Maybe he did like her, but he knows he can't give her what she wants maybe with regards to security or commitment. Ok. So, is he saying that he doesn't want anything serious basically? Is he? What does that even mean? 'Ok, Kim,' she said to herself. 'Can you do casual?'

What was she doing? Was she bargaining with herself because she wanted him? Or because she had never done casual before, but would she want to be serious with this HMP-bound man? Ok, ok, she pondered on. She started to think to herself. So let's get this straight. He is not husband material but he is a breath of fresh air. We are different but I enjoyed our chemistry so, so much with regards to physical touch and laughter. Basically, she was, without realising, bargaining with herself.

Unconscious about how she had just entered into his web in her own head, she texted him back to say, "I enjoyed the date so much, and that is all I want, so stop ruining it and be honest, and if you can't be honest, then just fuck off because I am tired these days".

He replied and said, "We will do something this weekend", and that is the response she received. He had ruined fucking it now. She'd already begun the overthinking and the analysing, and she would be watching his every move due to his ongoing disrespect. All she had wanted was to be and feel free. What fuckery, she thought.

Over the next few days, she did not hear from him. She was due on her period, bored, tired, hungry, and fed up with feeling sorry for herself as she did monthly. Luckily from following her menstrual cycle, at least she knew why she was feeling this way and what weeks she would be, and so was able to sit with it knowing what the upset was. Ping! "Hi, how are you, princess?"

She replied with an essay about her day, followed by another desperate message asking what he was doing in the afternoon. He replied with "Busy X". Kim's face rushed with a red of anger at herself. She shouldn't have responded in the first place to such a lame text. He hadn't been in contact and now he is texting days later with a crap message with no intention or interest, and she had responded like some desperate idiot, gratifying his super-inflated ego.

Fuck him, fuck him, fuck him, she thought. She told herself she didn't want him, to stop being a fool; she told herself firmly to forget this idiot of a man who is not interested in her or getting to know her. She was feeling drained and hurt and was that what she wanted for herself? No, she thought. Over the next few days, her energy switched to forget him, and she did. She concentrated on herself, her hobbies, and her daily life. She received a message from him, ignored it, and another message, ignored it. 5 messages later, still ignored it.

She couldn't have somebody fooling her around; she was too tired, weak, vulnerable, and didn't deserve any ill feelings in her life. 'Take your own medicine, you horrible cunt,' she beamed to herself. She knew that if he made the right effort and wanted to know her, she would be smitten with him, but for now, she would mirror his effort, which wasn't a victory for her really, entering into games with him. She would experiment with all the dating advice that she had read over the months.

She mimicked his behaviour over the days. If he gave her crumbs, she gave him crumbs; if he rang, she would cut him short like he cut her short.

Saturday came and it was pouring rain. The depression was real. She binged on chocolate, take-aways, crisps, and biscuits. Smoked roll-ups one after the other whilst looking at the dreary rain running down the window. In deep thought, she started thinking about Lee, her ex. She wondered if he was with anybody, if was he putting his new person through what he put her through. 'Of course, he is,' she smiled to herself. Poor fucker, whoever he has ended up with, she thought.

She thought of the magic she had shared with Lee and the pain in her stomach began as all through that magic he had been deceiving her, cheating on her, stealing from her. She quickly changed her thoughts so as to not spiral into the abyss of thinking and at that very moment, her e-mail notification sounded. Automatically, she knew it was Lee. It was like she had a sixth sense and when she was thinking about him, he was thinking of her. It had always happened.

Like some weird telepathic connection that they had with each other. Therefore, she believed in spirituality and energy so much. Whenever she thought of people, they would appear whether in town or shopping or wherever. "Hi, shit ass, are you ok? I am thinking about you a lot recently". Her heart sank immediately. Initially, she was sort of excited but then she had a scared feeling. Fuck, she thought. I am so over him, but for some reason, I feel so hopeless and weak.

They swapped numbers and that same helpless feeling carried on. She felt powerless again. She had in a way understood addicts really. It was all a mind fuck. Was he her soulmate and therefore no matter what, he will not leave her life? Souls connect and her and Lee's souls connected maybe stronger than anything logical and human. She used to lay with him and feel so at peace. She would think if she died at that moment, she would be at peace in his arms.

When they hugged and kissed, they would both venture into another world, it felt like a blanket of warmth washing over them—but then years later, Kim would know she was so susceptible to people's energy that she was actually feeling the effects of his heroin use as it transcended to her. He told her he was coming to see her at the weekend and sent her the coach booking confirmation.

It just seemed to overtake her, and it weirdly just picked up just where it left off and happened in a flash. He video-called her, he was being a bit erratic, and his eyes were the same old sleepy eyes, struggling to stop themselves from rolling to the back of the head. He was at a hostel in London for homeless people. She felt safe that he was out of Leicester. She was now wishing to God he hadn't contacted her. It had taken every morsel of strength to remove him from her life.

Her phone message notification pinged. "What time can I take you for breakfast?". She recognised Big Joe Joyce's number. She had a gleeful feeling. Fuck them both, she thought. Both are out to destroy me, so fuck them. She had been a good woman for so long. She was so loyal and devoted, and so she decided to just keep herself busy. When one was ignoring her, she would just go to the other. She felt a bit nervous though.

She knew if she would spread her interest elsewhere, then her value would go up with Mushy or Lee as when you're not interested, people want you and when you want them, they don't want you. In this case, Kim really did want Mushy but he was only using her for his ego. So, she was a bit fearful that Mushy now would get interested, but fuck him. He had already shown his true colours, he didn't want her. She would solely carry on and see how it all unfolds. She didn't have anything better to do romantically.

She at least wished at that moment that one of them would be financially stable so she could have some sort of benefit.

It was Saturday evening around 6pm. Kim had staved off last week's bad health by attending fitness classes and eating correctly. Her well-being was back on track and she was really looking forward to a night in and preparing for her date tomorrow morning with Mushy, but also not getting her hopes up because 99% he probably will ghost her like he normally did. Her message notification pinged, and it was Zack. "Hi, can I come and chill at yours for a few hours as I'm a bit down".

"Yes, of course, but I need to be in bed for 9:30pm as I want to be fresh as I have a date tomorrow morning. You want to go for a walk up Bradgate Park if you're feeling low? Get some fresh air? I will pick you up". She arrived at his and he was in the bath. Typical Zack, why can he never just be ready, she thought. She sat in the living room waiting and becoming agitated, wishing she had ignored the message and she could be home now in her PJs fresh out of the bath with a cup of tea and tv for the evening.

He came downstairs in a beautiful shirt and skinny jeans and started to pull on some purple shoes. Kim looked him up and down and asked him, 'Why are you getting dolled up for a walk around Bradgate Park? We're not going dogging, you know.' He smiled and Kim thought to herself, God, he is awfully quiet. His face started to almost droop to the floor.

'I have had space cakes,' he said. Kim smiled and thought that he must have a date after or something and didn't think much more of it. They arrived at her house and he sat on the sofa head on the phone. It seemed just so odd.

'Come on then, shall we go for a walk?' She said. Zack started to laugh and as he did, the door opened downstairs and one of their best friends, Nuria, came bouldering in with a bottle of Jack Daniels and Gin. They retreated to the kitchen and out came two bags of cocaine. Kim's heart sank. All she had wanted to do was to go to bed that night. She was baffled as to why he had done this.

She knew she had to get them out somehow. The thought of a party until 5am was freaking her out. It was the last thing in the world she wanted but now with two of her besties, how would she handle this? It was so awkward. Kim knew that she was easily steered and started to immediately battle herself. This is the reason why she had cut everything off as she didn't want any outside influence and if that meant losing people then so be it. For an hour, Zack was on at her to have a drink.

She knew it was harmless of him, she knew what it was like to want to party, and she would have been the same egging on any Tom, Dick, and Harry to drink with her or do a line. Nuria blessed Kim with the words she had to go at 22:30. It was now 20:00 and she had succumbed to a lager and a small line of coke the size of her fingernail, and even had pretended to sniff most of it just to shut Zack up. She started to merrily join in but in the back of her mind was still the anger and the will to try and control the situation.

Kim's phone video caller rang, and it was her sister, Reena, who she hadn't seen in a few months as that was another person she drank with. Tipsiness had kicked in and she was inviting Reena and Reena's friend, Jimmy, to the house for a few drinks. She stated it would only be until midnight as she had to get up on a date tomorrow—cringing at herself that the goalpost had now moved to midnight. Reena turned up and thanked God she did as it had helped the situation.

Kim told Zack her sister couldn't see the drugs; she'd tell the family, etc. It was bullshit and Reena would not have cared but it was a good plan. He had to hide the cocaine and go and take it in the bathroom and he wasn't going to have the opportunity to offer Kim some now, as if it had been just the two of them after Nuria left, she knew she would be telling them godawful words: "fuck it".

After an hour, Kim regained control of her mind by downing water and sobering up the tad tipsiness that had engrossed her. She turned the music off and started cleaning up, and after she requested firmly that everybody leave, she lay down on her bed with a wave of relief that the evening hadn't gone down a slippery road and she was going to be ok for her date tomorrow.

As she made away down the country roads again, she felt the familiar feeling of excitement. As she walked into his trailer, he was still in bed, and he summoned her to come and lie down for an hour snooze before breakfast. He too had been out and so it was such a relief to have another hour of sleep and a bonus of sleeping in his arms. She took her clothes off and climbed into bed. He stirred and grabbed her and pulled her tight into his embrace. It felt so warm and loving, and yet again, Kim just melted into his huge arms. It felt euphoric.

Their presence with each other was so natural, considering this was only the second time they had met, it was so comfortable and relaxing. They both drifted off into a euphoric slumber. After a while, they stirred and he turned to her, looked her straight in the eyes, and told her she was beautiful. The power of his bright, piercing, icy-blue eyes was overwhelming. Her stomach started doing somersaults and her passion took over.

He made her feel so good about herself, she didn't doubt his sincerity, but he had such a boyish charm, she knew he could put a smile on any woman's face, she was sure of that. She wanted him to relax and to please him, so she passionately got on top of him and let herself go whilst holding him down. She wasn't worried about what she looked like or what she might come across like; she held his neck with one hand and looked at him directly in his eyes as they watered and went to the back of his head.

She wasn't on contraception but was using her menstrual cycle and wasn't ovulating at the time, so she was hoping this method would work.

They both collapsed and went back to sleep until 11:30 and she awoke to him bringing her a coffee. He said he had booked breakfast for 12:00. They arrived at a pretty fishing lake with log cabins and a nice greasy spoon café, and after a week of health and a marathon sex session, she was so pleased to have fry up. He was such a gentleman, holding the door for her, and being super attentive, and they looked at each other lovingly with long stares. The laughter flowed and they were at ease with each other.

It started to pour down with rain and she could see the disappointment on his face as he had obviously planned a nice walk and perhaps to sunbathe. She could see him thinking in his head about what to do. Kim put him at ease and asked if they could just go to his and chill out with him, to which he looked relieved and agreed. On the way home, he said he had to stop at his mum's to drop her some weed off and he would like to introduce me.

Kim entered the bungalow and immediately liked the woman sitting in the chair with her dressing gown on with a big spliff in her mouth, two black cats, the same as her, and a picture on the mantelpiece of two rottweilers, which Kim had always dreamt of having as they were her favourite dog. There were boxes of medication stacked high on the table and she proceeded to take her tablets with a big swig from a can of Stella.

Kim was laughing to herself as she was old but not elderly looking. If she had seen her in the street, she wouldn't have thought that she would be a weed head. After some pleasantries, she pulled her dressing gown off and asked Kim if she liked her new top. It was a neon yellow and pink army pattern crop top and she had these huge boobs stuffed into them. Kim shrieked with laughter.

'You've had a boob job!' She exclaimed. 'They are 20 years old, these girls are.' She looked at Mushy and he was smiling and watching as they interacted. They left and headed back for another "snooze".

Monday came and the sinking feeling entered Kim's soul. Tears filled her eyes and her body tensed up as she started the day opening her e-mails, dreading the inbox full of queries and problems that she did not have the energy or brains to solve. She knew so many people had it worse, and she hated the fact she seemed like a spoilt brat, moaning that she had a secure job and some stability. She hated the control the system had over her. The fake, earth-destroying economy.

Of course, the comfort of heating and clean water on tap were absolutely fantastic inventions, but she was sure that the creative, wonderfully genius people who had invented it all didn't do it to make people trapped into a soul-destroying, fake, systematic life. Everything was about business. She hated business. Customer service, policies, procedures. It was all so inhuman and sheep-like.

She played podcasts and life talks on YouTube from the likes of Jordan Peterson, Sadguru, Joe Rogan, Russel Brand, and Nicholas Christakis, who were, like her, becoming ill in the ever-controlled, left-wing, politically correct world. She was sick of being told what to think, feel, and be. Anyhow, she cracked on and was stuck in the oppression of work whilst constantly thinking of a way out. She had been a lap dancer in a previous life and had escaped the system up until the ripe old age of 30.

All jobs were the same to her, so it didn't matter what job she would do, they would all make her feel the same. She contemplated asking Mushy to put her to work as a drug dealer but knew the money was not worth it nowadays; it was the same money that she was bringing in probably. She then moved on to thinking of being a honey trap but she wasn't sexy enough. She only had the nice girl next door look and not the looks of a woman that a man would lose his shit over.

Besides, she was far too honest for that and would fold at the slightest interrogation.

Mushy had arranged to see her on the Wednesday. She was smitten with his effort after Sunday and after seeing him use his tiny 1990s burner phone with the use of only one eye, she understood why he wasn't texting more interesting messages back to her (So that is what she said to herself to comfort the red flags). Kim had a sense he was scared in a way. He seemed guarded but when together, the love element was clearly there.

She was confused and wanted to clarify to him to not be scared, and just go with the flow and stop playing games. He had kissed her on the forehead on the Sunday, and said, 'This relationship is nice,' and so she was trying to decipher if he was saying "relationship" moving forward or "relationship" as in "arrangement". She decided that he had probably meant the latter and so buried her excitement.

She wouldn't be able to have casual sex, it just was not in her. She needed build-up, respect, compatibility, and a bond. He was giving her that, so she couldn't argue about a part-time thing for now.

She had totally forgotten about Lee and he messaged saying not to forget about the weekend. Her heart dropped in her belly and she started to cry a little bit as she felt so guilty and shameful like she had been cheating on Mushy or something. Mushy had been so beautiful to her and there was no way after what he was currently showing her that she would be disloyal to him.

She sent a message to Lee saying that she would always love him forever in this life and the afterlife, but she could not see him; it would be pointless to go back to square one all over again. She pressed block feeling so sad for Lee, but it was for the best for his hopeful recovery, and for her recovery also, as there was no way she could be liaising with two men at the same time.

She loved Lee and would not want to hurt him, even though he deserved it and she felt intensely loyal to Mushy at that moment and couldn't see herself sexually or romantically with anybody else.

Wednesday came and she was once again driving happily down the country roads. It was 3pm and he was not back yet from some random job he had got for the day. The trailer was open and it was 30 degrees heat. She sat on the sunbed outside and her whole body relaxed. She was in the middle of nowhere and the peace overcame her once again. She could see herself living here. She would grow some food and live basic without any responsibility, barbecue outside, and enjoy the freedom.

There was no electricity or running water so she would have to join a gym nearby to use their steam room and showers every day. She then came back down to earth with a bang as she thought what winter would be like. Freezing cold, no hot baths, having to boil water on a pan. The ideology suddenly turned from a dream into a nightmare and she smiled at her airy-fairy imagination. He arrived home and gave her the biggest ever welcome.

He pulled her up off the sunbed, took her head into his hands, looked her in her eyes, and said, 'How did I get you?' Kim's legs nearly collapsed from beneath her just because of the intensity of his eyes and mannerisms, and the power that he had over her. He grabbed her and said, 'Come, let's go for a walk.' They drove to a green space area that Kim knew from cycling the route and he would go fishing there. She wished she had bumped into him before.

Kim once again was grateful for his effort. He never let her pay for anything and she could see that it was outside of his comfort zone arranging dates and so on. She appreciated the gesture of him trying. They walked into the meadows and took a dip in a shallow lake. They kissed and laughed, and could not keep their hands off each other throughout the entire time. Of course, Mr Charming stopped and talked to every passer-by and she watched as their faces lighted up and he warmed their hearts with his zealous personality.

Kim was the total opposite. She was introverted and couldn't stand small talk. It was "eyes down, headphones in, don't want a conversation about the weather, thank you" with Kim. They got in the car and on the way to go and get food, he said, 'Let's pop in to see my brother.'

Fuck, fuck, fuck, Kim thought. Her social anxiety kicked in and she was fully aware that by now, she looked dishevelled from all the sunbathing, roiling around on the grass, and that fresh face out of the bath, no makeup look had disappeared a few hours back.

He picked up the energy on her face and said smiling, 'It is just 10 minutes, don't worry.' Kim had started to get used to him dragging her round from pillar to post now. He was just that sort of person who filled his hours being busy, not stopping, busy doing nothing. It was normal behaviour but Kim was so solitary and all the social interaction even with him was a battery drain.

Kim took a deep breath as they approached the door and she felt herself switching into her lap dance character but was finding it difficult to gain confidence as she wasn't glammed up with a protective face of makeup and clothes to help. Fake confidence, she whispered to herself. He entered the full house, bolshy, and disappeared laughing and full of conversation into a busy kitchen full of men. Kim sat on the settee stiff and awkward.

A girl appeared, her energy was very warm, and she sat on the sofa with Kim, and to her relief, it was a pleasant interaction. They left around 9:30 and Kim beamed to herself in the car at the fact that Mushy had really wanted to introduce her to his family, which surely after his mum and now his brother was this him showing her something? They went and got a Thai takeaway and went back to the trailer, and as Kim started to fall asleep, she felt so sad that the day was over. She wanted to do it all over again and feel all the loving warm feelings all over again.

It was Saturday evening and he had not contacted her since they had seen each other. She knew he had semi-stated their "relationship" as an "agreement" but she was confused as to his previously wonderful effort and the way they were together to now just be in the ghosted zone yet again. She thought at least a message would come through. She became stern with herself and told herself that it was just stupid escapism that she was in love with and not him.

She told herself that if he was all over her, she would probably run a mile and that she only wanted him because he was being scarce with her. She told herself to stop being a fool to believe his efforts as love and he was playing games with her and testing her, and so she would not chase him and refused to let herself indulge in fairy tale stories in her head. It is best this stupid fling is all forgotten about before I get hurt, she thought.

She woke up the next day and buried herself in work and began her mundane, dreary reality of busying herself with the gym, cycling, reading, and sitting at Costa listening to endless podcasts from King of The Sting and Theo Von, who made her laugh with their sheer immaturity that reminded her of her own teenage years banter. She had always been a lone wolf and she was her own best friend from childhood.

She had been lonesome for so long now, she wouldn't know even how to be with people unless she was drunk. She struggled in group situations such as meals out as she was so used to her own clock and if she went out for food, she would eat and then be so full, that she would rush home and lay on the sofa.

So having to negotiate in a group on splitting the bill and then staying an hour after food talking and managing to pluck up the courage to stand up from the table in front of everyone and announce that she was going home and say goodbye to everyone was really awkward for her. It was very sad, she knew this, but it was just how she was.

Her message notification pinged, and it was Lee. She had unblocked him previously as she didn't even want his number in her phone. She video-called him. They picked up where they left off as usual. Him being silly and making her laugh until her stomach hurt. He had lost his front teeth through drug use and had a brace with two front teeth attached, and he popped them out whilst talking to her making her laugh from her heart with his stupidity.

Her brother had committed suicide when he was 19. She was 18 at the time and so they were almost twins with their bond. The humour and laughter that they shared was what Kim had bonded with Lee over so much as he reminded her so much of him in terms of laughter and the stupid things he did. He started talking about coming back to Leicester as the job agencies had been contacting him crying out for welders. He asked her if he could stay with her for a month until he was sorted.

'Fuck off, Lee,' she said, smiling but with a deadly serious look of anger and panic. They got along so well but she had broken the spell from him a long time ago. There was no clean-living Lee. Even when he was clean for a few months here and there, the stress of him battling his addiction was not pleasant. She would never want to re-live or invite the darkest times of her life back in and she felt herself being annoyed that she was even talking to him. She finished the call and slept with dread because she knew Lee too well.

She knew he would just turn up at her doorstep if he wanted to. She hoped the distance would sway him otherwise. She knew he was clean in the hostel he was staying and working at because they did drug testing and if he failed, they would expel him from the programme, and he would yet again be homeless. She felt resentful that he was staying clean because, in her mind, she was angry that he wouldn't stay clean for their love.

Anyway, she thought. Fuck him. Even if he did come back to Leicester, my emotions are dead and buried for him relationship-wise. It was all in the past and she would never let him affect her life ever again. She wondered if he would ever be truly out of her life. Why does he keep popping up? she wondered. She squashed all thoughts and replaced them with the dread of work tomorrow and the fact that Mushy still had not contacted. She wondered if he had lost his phone.

Was he thinking about her? Would she hear from him again? She sure as hell was not going to text him and find out.

Lee turned up with his backpack on her doorstep. 'Don't worry, I am just visiting,' he said as he made his way into her house. He gave her a huge hug and they happily exchanged conversation over a cup of tea. They shared the bed cuddling and the time came when, because of her denying his sexual advances, he asked her if she had been with anybody else. She explained about Mushy and told him straight in not too much detail as to destroy him.

The next day, Lee went straight back to his usual self. Moody, withdrawn, and distant. Like the pull of drugs was unbearable for him to battle. He made his excuses at 8am in the morning to drop him at the coach station, but on the way past his old drug-haunting grounds, the pull was too unbearable for him. He told Kim to stop the car and drop him on Marwood Road as he wanted to visit an old friend.

Kim didn't question it. She knew his old dealers lived in this area and she just watched him as he left the car like a possessed wild animal that hadn't eaten for months.

She went back home and lay on the bed. Her chest was tight with almost post-traumatic stress at the reminders of what she had lived through with Lee. Her head started to spin, and tears rolled down her face as she relived the memories of being with him and living with his addiction. 6 years she had lived through his torture. She felt like she was having a heart attack and it was a familiar feeling that she had felt regularly when with him. From the first time, she found him with a needle stuck in his arm to everything that went with it.

He had burgled her mum's house, cheated, lied, manipulated, and stole her soul. She changed her thought direction and imagined herself with a man who looked after her heart. She would not be stressed, she could work part-time in a café, something easy as to not get bogged down with payroll calculations and difficult queries. Her only stress at work would be if somebody had a complaint about burnt toast or cold tea.

Her kitten came onto her pillow and started to kiss her face with its nose. Kim remembered when the kitten was only 5 months old, she had come home from work early, as she had checked her purse, her debit card was missing. She knew it was Lee who had taken it. She arrived home, bolted through her front door and ran up the stairs where she was greeted by Lee, who was collapsed in a drug-fuelled coma on the sofa with the kitten crushed underneath him squeaking with her last breath.

The kitten stayed near her head throughout that night and Kim appreciated the affection of animals and their beautiful company.

Kim was struggling again in the new week with the conform of 9-5 living. She started to obsess over free living, but even free living seemed to be for the rich. "I live in a yurt on my dad's farm" or "I converted my £60,000 RV and live on the road". She had investigated a few communities that had set up camps, but it was not her cup of tea to sit around in a circle with musical instruments, dancing around a fire barefoot.

She was spiritual but not that kind of spiritual. Surely there are people in communities who aren't long-haired, cult lovers. She searched on the internet and came across a website called "co-op housing" which from the website seemed as though it was self-sufficient living in a modern community interested in eco-living. It was in Derbyshire and not so far from her to go and visit.

She e-mailed the contact and the contact replied almost immediately to say there were some outhouses that were available in the autumn and to sign up for a group induction. Kim felt ecstatic that finally there may be a way out of her prison life. She wondered if to contact Lee who would be handy with maintenance, and he could be the exchange in return for living.

But the thought was soon squashed at the thought that after a week he would probably be robbing people of their belongings and then she would get kicked out with him solely for the association with him. She would do it on her own and she wouldn't even care if it didn't work out. She had to take a chance and her life was flying before her eyes. She was in love with Mushy and he was just messing with her about. She just needed an out before she went mad.

She was sad that she had stopped experimenting with life. She was only in her late 30s and she wanted upon her death bed to have tonnes of memories throughout life to look back on. She used to love herself for being wild, and free, and wanted to be that person again. She should have never bogged herself down with responsibilities and she hated herself as it would take nothing at all to get rid of these so-called responsibilities and go rogue again; but the older she got, the more fearful she became.

She looked at the website and imagined growing her own food, having chickens to lay the eggs, learning how to clean rainwater, and spending her time living as humans used to live. She imagined the long days in summer, every day to herself, wandering the meadows and streams, and looking after her animals and home. She read further on into the website and discovered that Co-op Housing (seemingly) was just another institution but on a smaller scale.

It was people running their own housing but without interference from the government—almost a left-wing cult on a smaller scale. Still, rent to pay/ownership/a leader. It seemed political which was even worse than hippy cults.

'Never fucking mind.' Kim cracked on with her payroll work. She sat and asked herself what she was actually trying to escape from. It wasn't Leicester that she didn't like; she liked where she lived, she had a variety of things to do, family to see, and friends to see. She could go on holiday if she wanted to (even though it would take an eternity to save up for a holiday but it was still doable), and go out to an array of different cultural restaurants.

She had access to every sport or hobby going. What was she trying to escape? Was a 9-5 that bad? The door came swinging open and Lee came waltzing in like an old, welcomed friend. Just need to stay for a few days, don't worry. I have a new job in London and a new room to rent to go with it but I can't move in until Monday so I need somewhere to stay as my hostel won't let me stay now I have a job.

She thought he may have been kicked out but she knew when he was lying or not and told him to go and make a cup of tea. He started emptying his bag out on the table frantically with his usually paranoid, jumpy energy. He had brought her a pack of pink wafers and he looked like a big goofy kid as he handed it to her. They sat with a cup of tea and just like the "old soul" friends they were, began to talk for hours in-depth and put the world to rights. Their compatibility was so high.

They could laugh, be deep, be silly, and were avid adventurers. They loved to go out into the woods and climb big trees and imitate sword fights with sticks like a pair of adult children. They would cycle for miles, finding beautiful woodlands that felt like nobody had ever set foot there. They would play fight in the fields in the newly grown corn and finally collapse in the sun for an afternoon snooze in the grass, meadows, or fields.

It was sad that the addiction was more powerful than her love for him, but that was all over now. Mushy had made sure of that and her love heart was only open to him. Lee tried again as hard as he could to initiate sex and she could see the pain in his eyes that night as he knew her love burned for another. Kim wondered why he even bothered with her. He could in her eyes have any girl he wanted to.

He was tall, dark, handsome, his body was big as well as his cock, and he had an incredibly attractive charm about him. Add in some HMP neck and finger tattoos and the mystery of him due to his addiction and Kim knew from her own experience how women felt about him and his God-like qualities.

He was a darn good lover as well and although she was repulsed by him due to his cheating, she knew what their sexual bond was before her becoming damaged goods at his hands, and it was the stuff of Gods. He loved to relax her. Kissing was passionate and he would massage every morsel on her to relax her head so she could let go sexually. She wondered why he was so desperate to re-kindle their sex life.

They went off the next day to the Peak District just for a small adventure before he went home and again started yet another new life somewhere else. They were discovering some caves and as they ran through the caves discovering all the nooks and crannies, as much as Kim loved Lee's company, she became sad at the thought of Mushy, wishing that it was Mushy who was with her discovering these things and bonding together and not her and Lee bonding over things for a non-existent future.

As she was thinking about Mushy, her phone pinged. "Messer", it said. She didn't recognise the number but knew it was him as she wasn't fucking with anybody else. She pondered on his message. He had not contacted her or been interested, and now wants to send a message calling her a "Messer". It was infuriating and she was worried about it as she had red-flag feelings that this behaviour was narcissistic and manipulative.

She couldn't resist replying. She knew she was replying to a death wish but chose to ignore the red flags as so many women do when dealing with alpha, narcissistic males with big dicks and a charm that sets them apart from the rest. "WTF. You have ignored me for 5 days and you want to call me a 'messer'.", she replied.

He messaged back, "I lost my phone. You know where I live, you can come anytime, and you haven't". Kim nearly fell into the bullshit of his words but dissected the information he was relaying to her, and she wasn't having any of it. How did he text her if he'd lost his phone and also his boss, mum and friend all had her number, so if he wanted to talk to her, he would have contacted her through them to at least inform her of the situation. It was heartbreaking.

She was falling for this man who she thought had shown her true love and now he was revealing himself as a narcissist, getting off on trying to psychologically twist things and mess with people's emotions. Or was she again thinking too deeply into things? Was he taking time to decide on her and now he wants her? Or "You best not be with any other man.", he messaged her. Kim looked over at Lee and laughed.

No, just playing husband and wife, she thought. She would never have messed up even in her friendship with Lee if Mushy wanted her. She would be with Mushy if he wanted her but he didn't, so fuck him. Kim dropped Lee at the coach station and yet again, they embraced for another new beginning for now.

It was Tuesday and Mushy had said he wanted to see Kim. He mentioned taking her to the meadows where they had one of their first dates. She biked up to the meadows and rang his phone to see where he was but he never answered. Here she was again with this confusion. Giving him the benefit of the doubt and questioning herself and her instincts to only now be stood waiting for him and he wasn't responding. She started to uncontrollably have tears flow down her face.

She tried so hard to stop them as people were walking past but they carried on flowing. She was yet again a victim of this odd male behaviour. She was sure females did it too, but her experience was with the male species, so she did not wander about the female behaviour. Why do people like toying with and hurting people? This is what she could not understand.

She took a deep breath, wiped her tears and cycled so hard and fast on the way home whilst listening to gangster rap on her headphones. She needed to release these stupid feelings and she was so mad at herself for yet again falling for this stupid idiot's games.

The next day through the post some photos arrived through her letter box of her and Mushy that she had previously ordered a few weeks back. She had weakness in her bones upon looking at them and wanted him to have them purely to try and secure a reaction in him to want her. Maybe if he could see her face, it would trigger him to want her. It was desperation and the rejection he had shown her that had triggered almighty feelings almost to try and prove she was worthy to him.

It was really bad that she was losing control and started to think why she was engaging in this toxic behaviour. She made a pact to herself to drop the pictures off at his trailer whilst he was at work and then just leave it as a nice memory for them both. She knew this was both desperate and tragic but it was like an energy was forcing her to do it. Like she had no control. She made the one last drive down the country roads and smiled thinking this is all for the best, leave the photos of them with him and leave it in God's hands.

Follow her own path and stop getting emotionally involved unless he would properly invest. She sprayed her perfume on his pillow like some psychopath out of a horror movie. She was so relieved that he hadn't been there. She sat on his bed, put the picture of them both on the mirror and sighed with relief to close the chapter. She had one last look around and smiled at the short but powerful romance she had encountered with him.

She realised it was around 4pm and she should make a move and she ran to the car. As she was driving off, he pulled up with a car full of people. He looked straight at her in an angry way and she went bright red and carried on driving. She was absolutely dying inside now at the realisation of what she had done. He was going to walk into his trailer with all his friends to see silly photos and she was going to come across as an absolute idiot, which is what she was.

She started to laugh and thought who fucking cares. Later that evening, her phone pinged. 'Why are you messing me around? I lost my phone, and you haven't been to see me?'

Once again, the fuckery of it all set into play. Again, if he had lost his phone, how did he have her number? Kim chose to ignore the logic of herself and yet again, chose excitement and unhealthy fuckery at his request as he had told her to come back up to his "now". There she was back on the country road on her way back to him.

As she walked in, he looked in distress and kept saying "You're a messer, you're a messer". It was almost as if he believed his own lies. He grabbed her and kept saying, 'Listen, I have feelings for you but don't have my life, please don't have my life.' Kim had every red flag in her mind, body and soul trying to wave at her, but she was pretending that she couldn't see them and looked the other way instead, even knowing she was in serious danger with this one.

Lee was an addict and a manipulator, but his vile behaviour was to hide his addiction. This man was messing with her for fun. Enjoying making a fool out of her, trying to mess with her head, and she was dumbing down to be with him. She kept telling herself that there wasn't a deep bond with him and as they were not together officially, that she could and would just keep dabbling just for the thrill and excitement of it, but in reality, she wanted love, she wanted a deep connection, a partner in crime and a ride or die.

So what was she doing here? Whilst he was spouting his fake words, it was almost like she was disconnecting from herself and watching herself and calling herself an idiot as she watched him spout out his lies.

Over the next few weeks, surprisingly things turned around. Mushy was so hospitable and whizzed her around meeting more family members. She loved his family members; they were all down-to-earth, common, and open.

They were her kind of people, unapologetically themselves. Authenticity is what Kim treasured in people the most. She didn't like any sort of formalities or etiquette. She accepted anybody as they were though, from whatever walk of life they may be from.

But these people were her favourite as they were themselves from the get-go. You could just go into their homes and make yourself at home and be yourself. Kim felt bad that she felt like she couldn't introduce Mushy to her family (and quite frankly, didn't want to for his sake). Her family was normal and the idea of sitting through a meal doing small talk with Mushy was just a no.

Mushy swore every 2 seconds as did most of Kim's friends and she could imagine her mum's face at Mushy turning up in his tracksuit with a spliff hanging out of his mouth, swearing at every other word. They had driven down to Wiltshire as Mushy wanted Kim to meet his adoptive mum. After 5 minutes, Kim felt like she was looking at her own mother. They were similar in every manner, the way they talked, the etiquette down to the hyacinth bouquet act that would gradually wear off after a few whiskeys.

Maybe Kim was a bit harsh on people as most people did have social etiquette and they had to do the small talk and vibe each other out before letting their true sides out. But Kim always watched the same thing unfold time after time—after a few drinks, everyone letting loose and being themselves and she seethed in her head "Well, why didn't you all just be yourselves from dot one".

They went to a restaurant and Kim was giggling inside as Mushy was his usual loud, brash, and unapologetic self. Kim was watching Mushy's mum's body language and she could see her cringing inside as Mushy was filling his mum in (very loudly) on what his last stint in prison had been like and how he had been stabbed and was running a few lads on the wing. The very nice and very well-to-do lady, who was the personified version of Kim's own mum, was suffering in silence with embarrassment.

She could see her drinking more and more wine to get through the pain. Kim then watched Mushy and wondered herself why all her friends and lovers were mostly loud, confident powerhouses that commanded attention, and people adored them and loved them off. She wondered why they always seemed to seek her out and they always ended up together. Kim was in no way an arse lick.

She was deadly confident in herself and perhaps they were attracted to each other for their similarities of being powerful and strong but were totally different in how they achieved or had these qualities.

As the weeks passed, the energy between them became a tad awkward due to Kim having pacified herself so much to be with him that the overstepped boundaries were starting to seep out of the makeshift bandages. She so wanted to connect on a deeper level but was finding him avoidant. Their interactions were based on her turning up at 7pm at night after an exhausting day at work and for him to arrive home at 8pm, and have acrobatic sex which unconnected her mentally, and she had started to switch off a little.

Kim was so incredibly stressed from her job and then after work, the effort it took to do her hair, tan, and nails and look good for him, and feel such a build-up of excitement only to have fast vigorous sex immediately without any connection or build-up was becoming a worry to her. She fancied him so much and he had such a nice cock, and the sex was so, so good. Probably the best she'd ever had if it was auto-tuned more into connection, but at this point, she was feeling unconnected.

It was becoming excruciatingly awkward after the butterflies were turning into familiarity and her pussy was feeling scared of being approached by his huge fingers rubbing her clit so hard that it was painful. With a little massage and some gentle but firm touch, it would have been such a perfect build-up, but no matter what she did, she just couldn't make him relax or go deep and build something together.

It was avoidant, pornographic, and immediate what he wanted, and so the tension from her long day at work and then not having that tension relieved and more tension added on at the sexual awkwardness and incompatibility was even more stressful. She felt sad as he was so beautiful and had everything she desired. She also became fearful as she was starting to be a bit sexually closed off and became intensely paranoid that him not desire her as she was boring in bed because she couldn't relax.

Every time they connected, the awkward energy was intensifying. She knew that if she had the chance to even see him in the afternoon at the weekends, then it would be a whole different story as she would be relaxed, not tired and in the mood, but she was only ever getting to see him at bedtime after a huge meal at the end of a mentally draining day.

She was pleased that on the rare occasion she had caught him in the afternoon, they had amazing breakthroughs and they connected again when she looked him straight in the eye as she was coming on his cock. But why could he not have enjoyed that and know that was the right time for them to have sex and quality time? She had told him numerous times and he had listened and delivered on the breakthroughs mentioned, but all in all, the same remained.

She still adored his touch and his love. He was attentive and sweet, and he made her feel incredible. She wanted to make him feel like he was incredible but felt like a failure because she couldn't. She had dominated him at times and pinned him down, forcing him to relax, and sucked his dick deep, slow, and firm whilst massaging his legs and thighs, and putting all her sensual energy into him, avoiding anything frantic, hard and fast.

She was trying to show him what she wanted. She would relax him so much and she knew he was deep in his thoughts as his cum would just spurt deep in her throat and as she swallowed it all, she loved knowing that he was a hard one to get to relax and was glad that he could with her. Their morning sex was the best. She would pretend to be asleep as his huge, hard dick gently slipped in her and it was slow and deep, and she felt like she was having an orgasm at every stroke. Maybe they should just stick to morning sex, she thought.

It was getting cold as it was late August and it had been a terrible summer with not much sunshine at all. Kim had a long, exhausting week at work as per usual and she was so looking forward to seeing her Mushy. He had invited her on Friday and he had said for her to turn up and wait for him, as somebody had robbed a large stash of drugs from him and he needed to go and sort it.

Kim winced at the thought of turning up and waiting in a cold trailer with no electricity as she didn't know how to work the generator. She said to him, 'Do you want to leave it tonight, babe, as you seem busy,' thinking he might end up having a few drinks with it being Friday, but he said he wanted an early night and to go see him. Perfect, she thought, being so tired herself.

She made herself fresh and it was 6pm but he hadn't texted her. She thought she should be productive and instead of waiting around, she should go to the gym to let off some pent-up work stress. She smashed the CrossFit machine for an hour and at 7:00pm, there was still no text. She stressed and did some floor work on the mat, and at 7:30pm, still no text. Her anxiety started to spike so she rang him and he said he would be home in an hour.

Ok, she might as well have stayed at home but she freshened up as the drive was 45 minutes, so they could arrive at the same time. The country road she was familiar with was now dark, cold, and eerie. She arrived and was hoping to see his trailer with the lights on and finally go in to lay down in the warm and chill, but to her disappointment, there was nobody home.

She sat in the car with the heater on and engine running thinking how much she would love to be in bed now at home with a cup of tea, chocolate, and her cats cuddling up with her watching a film snuggled up in her dressing gown. She sighed and dialled his number. He answered and seemed manic and said that his brother had been arrested and he was at his brother's house changing the locks for whatever reason.

He sounded sniffed up and she could hear people in the background, so Kim put out an olive branch and said she would go home and leave it so he could sort out his business. She thought he would be pleased but he switched and started shouting that she should be by his side. Kim thought it was sweet and of course, said she would wait in the car for him as he was only 10 minutes away so he could come and pick her up. Then they will go back to his brother's and stay at his as he needed to look after his brother's dogs.

45 minutes later, Kim was still sitting in her car cold and tired. No phone call or text and she texted him to say, "I'm going to leave tonight, babe, and go home. Hope everything is ok. I don't know what's happening so thought it best I go". As she drove out his road, she got to the first corner and he came speeding up. He looked at her and he knew it was her. She honked her horn very hard and long numerous times but he carried on driving and didn't stop. Why didn't he stop? He knew it was her. It just didn't feel right.

She so badly wanted to go home but what if she was overreacting? What if his phone died or something further had happened? So she sped the car around and headed back. As she pulled in, another van pulled in at the same time with his friend in and she realised he had come back to arrange to meet his friend and had fobbed her off a long time ago even though she had put the olive branch out to go home earlier. He looked uncomfortable and said, 'Oh, was that you honking your horn at me?'

Kim absolutely fucking died inside and her stomach sank at the blatant, direct rejection but she was almost frozen as to do or say anything. She followed him in the trailer as she was so confused by his words earlier of wanting her by his side but now she was being faced with a different reality of rejection. He and his friend were both coked up and they started chatting about roadman shit. She looked at them both smiling sarcastically with her bitch face as they went on about drugs and gold.

Kim had travelled the world on her own, learned another language and seen some fucked-up places, and so the talk of the local boys with their man bags and Moschino tracksuits left her in repulse. They'd be crying in their fucking bandanas if she threw them in the middle of South or Central America. Not Mushy though, Mushy was hard as fuck. He wouldn't go down for nothing or nobody. Knowing him, he'd go to the countries and everyone would lick his arse just like this lad was doing right now.

Luckily, his friend had a wife and a baby to go home to, so made his excuses and left. Mushy sat there looking disappointed at the sight of her. They drove to his brother's house, and it was now midnight. Mushy went and sniffed a line of coke that had been left on the side and appeared from the kitchen with snot running down his nose. 'What would you do if I went to prison, babe? Are you ride or die?' If only Mushy knew how to ride or die she had been the last 6 years with Lee. She was not in a position to be a ride-or-die woman.

She wanted to say yes, if you support me financially, make me a housewife and look after me, then yes. She wanted to say, 'Yes, look after me financially, so I don't have to work and I'll be a ride or die whilst sucking your dick and washing your arsehole if you requested it. But as I am working, paying my own bills, and dealing with the mental health of being stressed from work and holding myself afloat, do you think I have any energy or love at the end of that to be someone's ride or die if they aren't showing me that back?'

It was all getting bullshit now. All this fucking talk and no action. They went to bed and embraced, and the touch connection that she had been waiting for all day rushed over her, followed by rough, quick, acrobatic sex for hours on end whilst he was on his coke buzz, with which he was frustrated to not make her cum, but still didn't understand it would have only taken some sweet words and a loving build-up for even just 5 minutes and her pussy would have been more than happy to cum all over him.

But instead, it was immediately attacked with vigorous, hard, painful rubbing. She was mentally fucked and energetically drained in the morning. They cleaned the house and Kim asked if he could drop her back to her car as understandably he was already on the phone with his mate organising to meet up for breakfast as a hint for Kim to fuck off. She felt humiliated and rejected again and the ride home was as uncomfortable as her sore pussy. She practically ran out of his car into hers and as she drove past him, he blew her a kiss.

As much as she had wanted to get away from him as soon as she turned the corner, she started to miss him. How could she be missing trauma? What was she missing? The experience that she wanted that she had never received. Was her body just remembering the 5 minutes of warm euphoric cuddles wrapped up in his arms and dismissing the other 12 hours of hell that had just gone on? She baffled herself.

It was Tuesday and a payday. She checked her online banking, and after all her bills were deducted, she took a deep sigh at the £12 left spare to live on for the rest of the month. How would she pay for petrol, cat food, her food, and any other basic living costs? She knew most of the single, young population who lived on their own lived like this and so she tried to think positively and told herself that at least the bills were paid and she had a roof over her head.

She would just have to struggle and occupy herself with free things such as the gym, walks, and cycling, and go and visit her family for dinners and if necessary, find a food bank. She pondered over the fact that she could not survive like this much longer and thoughts of herself getting older and still being in this situation were scary. She was so tired at the age of 37, what would she be feeling like at 60 years old?

She battled with the thoughts and made a suicide pact with herself—as soon as she couldn't be independent, and she of course would have nobody to take care of her, she would top herself somehow. She had already researched how pure helium could kill her instantly but she wouldn't know where to find pure helium for sale. She moved her thoughts on what she could do for extra money.

She thought of a practice called Chinese cupping, whereby you placed suction cups on the muscles and it pulled up the blood for better circulation, relieving aches and pains in the specified area. She had a fold-up massage bed but she was apprehensive about doing it as if it was male clients, she knew they would of course see her as a sexual object and try their luck and she didn't even want to deal with that nonsense. Plus she would be doing it from her home and so clients would know where she lived, but what fucking choice did she have.

She needed something, a little extra earner. She had tried dog sitting but work had pulled her back in the office 3 times a week, so she wasn't able to do that anymore. She thought about going back to lap dancing but she was so unconfident in herself that there was no way she could go prancing around on show like an extravert, exuberating confidence like she had once falsely had. The only way dancers make money is through confidence.

You could be Jennifer Lopez in looks but if the dog sat next to you had confidence, then guaranteed she would be the one taking home the money. That is another thing she hated about herself. She was confident in herself, going about her own business and felt attractive and healthy but the down days were a killer, and she hated having to interact with people when inside she was dying with self-loathing.

The thought of staying up until 6am lap dancing and having to talk to people reminded her of why she used to drink Brandy, otherwise how else would she walk around smiling all through the night when naturally she went to bed at 9pm and relished in early morning rises, fresh, and ready to take on the day. She knew that was not an option she would ever consider again unless forced by gunpoint.

Her phone pinged and she quickly grabbed it as she had been doing for days awaiting hopefully a message from Mushy. It was him, the message solely said, "Messer". She wasn't even angry or sad. She was numb at this point. She so desperately wanted to know why some people got a thrill out of trying to emotionally toy with somebody's feelings. She replied only with the word "narcissist" but regretted even replying to the text as he would likely not know what the word narcissist even meant.

He replied, "I don't know that one. Does it mean that you love me?". She did not respond and put the phone back in her bag. She felt a bit relieved as she knew he was trouble and she wondered how long it would be before he ended back up in prison anyway. He was 35 and did not seem to want to spiritually grow or mature into a real man with goals and to face himself as she had faced herself. He cowered away with alcohol and pills and Kim found that weak.

She did love his manliness and his outer strength but couldn't help being repulsed by someone so weak to hide away with tablets and alcohol and not be present in life and fight it. Her work colleague had figured she was talking to Mushy by Kim's gloomy face and said to Kim, 'You should find a nice guy.' Nice guy, Kim said in her head. Who wants a fucking nice guy?

Kim wanted a monster, but a monster who could have the capability to be a monster but didn't have to be because their strength and presence let people know not to mess. Kim wanted a warrior, a soldier. They sure would be nice to her, she did want that, but Kim didn't want a "nice guy", otherwise she would be with any one of the million guys that were after her. It was very mixed up. There weren't many options for women nowadays.

There were not many big, strong, manly men around and the minority of these men had the pick of hundreds of beautiful females. Kim asked herself why there were so many stunning women who fit the bill of what a man would want, yet where were all the big warriors, the soldiers, the action men that women secretly loved? They were a rarity and a rarity that Kim could and seemed to attract. She turned to her colleague and replied that this was her life path and that whatever will be, will be.

If she falls in love with a nice guy, then so be it but now this was her situation, and she would just watch it as the days unfold and see what happens.

Over the coming days, the darkness was once again the very real reality for Kim. She could make sense of it as she was due on her period but Mushy's rejection had made it all so much worse and had opened something in her that was not pleasant. She couldn't cope with work and the emotional trauma of being messed around and rejected, so booked annual leave immediately for a few days to try and recover emotionally through well-being at home.

Unfortunately for her, all she could do was lay in bed heartbroken. She turned her phone off and told the world to fuck off as she ate chocolate instead of nutritious food, swigged on endless mugs of lattes and hid away safely in bed watching TV with her cats on her pillow next to her head. After the 3rd day, she summoned her strength to go to the steam room and for a swim. Her eyes were puffy and she felt incredibly vulnerable.

The sort of vulnerable that if somebody asks you if you're ok with a concerned face you would burst into tears at the gesture of somebody being nice to you. She made her way to the steam room and felt instant relief with the heat and the steam ridding her of the built-up stress she had in her body and mind. A familiar face was in the steam room and he looked just as broken as she did.

He uninvitedly opened up to her that his marriage had broken down and he could not see his children, and as he was Muslim, he felt like a failure in his faith being divorced. He asked Kim what she wanted out of life and Kim replied that she didn't think like that anymore as plans never worked out. She said that she had fulfilled a lot of her goals with travel and now she just lived day by day and tried to be grateful for the little blessings.

More men entered the steam room and who Kim knew and often had banter with and so she moved on quickly from the depth of their conversation to much more needed light-heartedness with the others. One of the men was talking and made a joke about his ex and about women in general. The man with whom she had been previously talking, homed in on Kim with pure anger and hatred in his manner, and said, 'Yeah, like this one here. She's not a nice woman; she isn't married or does not want children. She's not a nice woman.'

The room went quiet at the awkwardness and Kim muscled up the strength to get some big dick energy and piped back to remind him that he wasn't married and didn't see his kids, so does that make him a horrible man. She got up from the steam room and jumped in the pool as a distraction so as not to burst out crying in front of everyone. When he came out, he walked over to her and apologised saying that he was angry and sad and that he should not have said the things he said; he was just stupidly lashing out.

Kim, of course, burst out crying and his face looked like his heart had broken that he had been so horrible to someone. She told him not to worry about it and that she too was going through a hard time and to think carefully next time as we are all going through tough times, and what if it was worse and the reason why she couldn't have children was a medical reason or what if her child had died. He should be more mindful in future.

At that, they both awkwardly exited, and Kim drove home once again to her safety net of bed, still in the position of being deep in old wounds of rejection that Mushy had so cruelly inflicted upon her. She thought maybe it was a blessing in disguise that all the emotion was flooding out of her and it would actually help that she is facing the reality of rejection and it would make her stronger.

Nobody goes through life without rejection and so this would help make her fierce and strong, and once again she would take any negative and overcome it and make it a part of her war wounds. She hoped that after such an emotional outburst for the last few days, tomorrow would of course be a new day with a fresh energy to it.

That evening, she looked at Lee's profile picture on WhatsApp. She pressed unblock and both were just online without typing for at least a minute seemingly in a trance. Kim broke the telepathic silence and sent the monocle man emoji. "Oh my God, I have been thinking about you all night and day", he wrote. "Please come and see me at the weekend. I have moved to Wimbledon and I have my own place now, well a room that costs £750 a month and a really good job".

He started to send her videos of the tree-lined streets, stating he had breakfasted every day at Bills Restaurant and his Nuffield Gym membership was £95 a month, and showing in pictures his 10 pairs of brand new £200 trainers neatly colour co-ordinated in a row at the end of his bed on the floor. Kim seethed a little at the fact not so long ago he had been using her SIM card that she unknowingly had included in the Virgin Media package when she first moved into her house.

He had stolen it and when she started to get bills over £100 because he had gone over the data cap, she had uncovered through talking to an advisor at Virgin Media that it was a SIM card that had been in use. So now here he is yet again—clean of drugs and doing well but his selfish self was not even offering a smidge of money towards the thousands of pounds now racked up that she had spent on him.

She remembered how much she had loved him and if he ever struggled, she was there like a loyal dog emptying her bank account for him to sort out his messes as she could not bear the thought of him struggling. Speaking to him and hearing about his new golden life was the last thing she needed to hear as she looked at the raggedy clothes she had had for the last 5 years.

Then the thought of going to London looking like a complete tramp whilst it was cold, and her only winter coat being ripped at the seams, so she just ignored him again as she only felt anger towards the selfish cunt.

The next day arrived, and she was still rather vulnerable, but okay to just get on with the day. She was in a deep thought mood and she, for some reason, was thinking about the selfishness of Lee and thought of her selfishness. When she was younger, she had a close group of friends whom she loved dearly but her own dreams of travel and life goals had made her quite distant and aloof whilst her friends were having the most important life events such as childbirth and marriage.

Now Kim was older and she felt sad as she realised now these were huge events and Kim was not there to support her friends through these events—partly because she didn't understand them at the time and took it as a pinch of salt as she was travelling the world, but now being older, she deeply regretted that at the time she didn't understand the importance of these events.

How much she would have liked to turn back time and be there for her friends like she should have been. As she was pondering the thought, one of the friends in her thoughts at that time appeared in a car in the car park next to her. This was always an occurrence—seeing people as she thought of them. The friend had 4 children, 2 dogs and 3 cats and had been living in a rented property for over 10 years.

The owner now needed to sell the house in the next 6 months leaving her friend no other option but to go to a hostel in the next few weeks. On top of that, her car had blown up. Kim offered in whatever way she could to help and begged her to not be shy about any help she needed. Kim would do anything and agreed, for a start, to help home one or all the cats until she was sorted. It was so nice that God had sent a small opportunity to rectify some of the guilt Kim had felt that day and it was nice to help in a small way.

Lee asked Kim if she was coming down but Kim excused herself and said she was having to look after her friend's cat. He said he would book a ticket to come and see her and she thought that it actually might be nice to have a home full of cats and some company from Lee to soothe and distract her pain from Mushy's rejection.

Lee once again was at her house and on the first day he was pleasant and nice to her as always. The conversation flowed and the laughter at his silliness was ever present, however by Sunday, the dark cloud had appeared over him like the devil had caught up with him and hung over his head like a death sentence.

After years of this dark presence that Kim had battled with, thinking it was her who had done something wrong or devasted that he could hate her so much, she now realised that he was just a hateful, spiteful person with demons deeper than anyone could have known. It was an entity within him so evil and moody, and the anger was brewing just beneath the surface ready to explode at any time.

Kim was not in love with him anymore, so watching it occur without the emotional attachment was refreshing. It used to destroy her and now she could see clear as day it was never her. This was who he was with or without drugs.

He went home on Sunday to both of their relief. It was a beautiful day and Kim felt happy that she was in her own company again. A new number appeared on her phone, and it of course was Mushy. 'No visit no? No, nothing? You just disappear again?'

By Tuesday, Kim was at his trailer. She explained yet again how she thought he was mugging her off and the rejection she had felt had been unbearable. She thought if she could keep explaining to him how he was hurting her by messing her around, he would stop doing it.

He said the same thing he always said—'If I lose my phone, just come here and see me. If I'm not here, I will be at my mum's or in prison, that is the only place I will be. I don't know what more to say to reassure you. I lost my phone and once again, you disappeared.'

Kim was battling whether to accept this guy was this simple to just turn up to his if he hadn't contacted her or again acknowledge the facts that if he had lost his phone, then how did he text her from his new number, or if his mum or friend had her number would he not text her from their phone just to at least inform her. She chose to ignore the hurt of reality and lied to herself with great difficulty that the next time this happened, she should just turn up to his trailer, right?

It sounded beneath her in so many ways, turning up like some little lapdog to somebody who was blatantly hurting her. She lied to herself a little further and told herself that men communicate straightforwardly and if this is what he was saying, then it was the straightforward truth and that he wasn't rejecting her, and next time she will just follow his direction like a good girl.

It was her fear of rejection and being in a fearful energy which was causing her pain and she should just realise that he was unpredictable and spontaneous, and accept their differences. She was a meticulous planner, detail orientated, and he was the complete opposite, so she would listen to what he said and act in a way that suited him more and see if that would help the situation.

She felt reassured with her new plan and that evening, she was safe in his huge arms with the feeling of liquid ecstasy running through her veins. It was quickly disrupted by his Aries Male energy to get hard and heavy immediately with sex without any build-up or sensuality whatsoever. She was in no mood for the gymnastics and cardio workout of it all and with all the feminine energy she had, she poured all her goddess-like energy to somehow overpower him.

She held him down gently and persuasively with kisses, licking his lips, and persuaded him non-verbally to stop struggling to take the power and be under control. Kim's heart, now feeling safe after her decision to believe him, could let go sexually and once again the sexual energy had returned, watching each other's eyes water and roll back with pleasure.

A few weeks had passed and although Kim was happy in general with life, bar a few small ups and downs, she could not ignore the fact that money was so tight. She could not get out of her overdraft and each month on payday, the repayment was eating into all of her wages. It wasn't even a slippery rope anymore, she had let go of the rope and plunged straight into a swamp of crocodiles. She needed around £2000 to pay her overdraft off, plus all of her bills, not to mention the things that she would like rather than need.

She had sold a few possessions to try and put things right such as her X Pole that she hadn't used and a £200 coat she let go for £25 so she could afford petrol money to get to work. She needed some food shopping that week, so she sold her camera for £15. Enough is enough, she decided. Fuck it. She pulled out the massage bed and then proceeded to place an advert for a massage service, £30 an hour.

She figured 1 massage a day is £210 a week, £910 a month on top of her wages. She had thought long and hard (in a typical Capricorn fashion) to do this. As soon as the advert went live, her phone started to go insane. The men messaging her, despite the advert stating in bold capital letters THIS IS NOT A SEXUAL SERVICE, still believed it was a sexual services advertisement.

She knew from working in the tame side of the sex industry that men would have, in fact, ignored the capital letters and still pursued sex in the hope of it. She picked out 2 perspective clients from their profile pictures being on face value relatively normal looking and ones that she would feel comfortable with. She was being selective and she would not feel obliged in any way shape or form to do anything. At £30 an hour for a massage, she would certainly be able to smash down any of their dirty expectations.

As a lap dancer, she had charged £300 just for an hour to sit down in a private booth where all they got was a naked dance or most times they were so intoxicated, they would fall asleep. It would be easy as well as they were responding to her advert, coming to her home. It wasn't like she was competing with 30 other girls and having to make conversation and sell anything to them. Just one hour with no sales, late nights or drinks involved.

Easy. Kim loved massage, yoga, relaxation, and helping people de-stress, and she was falsely hoping that is what the advert would attract, but at a huge risk, she knew it was more likely to attract weirdos, murderers, rapists maybe. She became scared at the thought, but it was either to get out of debt quickly or lose her home, her peace, and her cats, and go back to her dad's house to live or rent a room. Fuck that, she thought.

Both sitting in front of a PC for 7.5 hours a day and massaging people who were thinking there could be possibly more were degrading, but at least the latter is a quick way to make extra cash. She printed out a booking calendar and started to sift through the hundreds of messages. She couldn't believe it. She could never be a brass but imagine the money you could earn if you had no feelings. Fair play to them, she thought. She booked her first appointment "David" at 16:00 for 1 hour.

She was surprisingly unbothered about the fact somebody was coming to her house to get naked, albeit with a towel to cover their bits, and she was going to massage them. It must have been her old job that had made her rather unbothered and blocked off. She didn't see herself as sexual and never understood why anybody else would either, so any advances or flirting went straight over her head anyway, so they can carry on fucking her in their head if they like.

It made no difference to her reality. The door knocked and as Dave entered through the hallway, she felt immediately at ease. She handed him the crisp, new white towel and instructed him to get undressed, and come upstairs in the towel when ready. He seemed nice but she knew these guys were going to try and get more, but she would just play dumb.

They read the advert so they should know it is not what they desire.

He was a mental health worker and Kim had previously worked in mental health for a few years. It turned out they both knew the same service users who were notorious to the agencies such as the crisis team. One of the clients was famous within the sector. She had been in care from her early 20s and was on par with Charles Bronson. She beat staff up, chased people with knives, smashed her accommodation up, and attempted suicide almost every week.

She was a huge, fat, 6ft tall Jamaican woman with no teeth. Kim had hated working with her but at least the woman liked Kim and almost understood her introverted personality, and had predominantly left Kim alone but abused the other staff instead. The hour flew by, and he left her a £10 tip as to did the next customer and the next customer. Kim was relieved the wheels were finally in motion but also a tad resentful that she had to do this to survive.

Therefore, she thought Mushy was wasting her time and a feeling of resentment fired in her belly. She chose a man like him because he seemed old-fashioned and masculine, and he should want to love and protect a woman. Why was she having to seemingly wait for him to look after her? It was not as if she would stop working and be totally financially reliant on him but she could at least be looked after, work part-time to help and stay at home, be a woman, and have the life she desperately wanted to have.

Now she was double in trouble by having a full-time job that was destroying her soul and she had to degrade herself in a sense by massaging for a living to survive. The next client arrived. A young ginger man who was pale and chubby. He was shy and awkward. When the massage was over, he turned around and his tiny 4-inch cock was sticking up through the towel.

He looked at her awkwardly and piped up the courage to ask if she did extras. Kim casually answered him and said 'No, it did say on the advert. Did you not see it in big capital letters?'

'I am sorry, it is just that I got them vibes,' he replied. Jesus Christ, Kim thought. She had a bath, got ready and rushed to see Mushy. She knew she had fallen head over heels for him; she felt a loyalty to him and felt like she belonged to him. Although, it was all a spiritual and love connection but outside of this realm of love, touch and cuddles, it seemed very difficult. There wasn't any deep conversation and he seemed so avoidant with planning anything together.

She wondered why he kept reeling her in if he wasn't serious about her. Kim had a wet pussy all day thinking about him, he was so beautiful to her. He looked like a man that God had made. His body, his deep voice, his raw soldier-like quality. He was a warrior to the bone. He had not evolved one bit and it was a rarity to have men of that calibre, albeit she was realising that also he was unreliable and dangerous. She was not going to lie to him.

She was dreading telling him about her day. She was hoping he would whisk her off her feet and go mad at her for having to do that and say that he would look after her and she wouldn't have to get an extra job to support herself. They would do life together and she could relax, and everything would be ok. He only replied with safety concerns and to make sure she texted him before and after appointments to know she was ok. She could see from his eyes he had detached from her and had a feeling she had been demoted immediately.

Which was understandable. There was nothing in what she was doing but from his point of view, she could see his head spinning at the thought of her touching other men. She didn't have a choice to stop it now though. He was not offering her security and so she had to do life by herself.

A month had passed, and the massage business had taken off, more than Kim had ever expected. She had paid off her overdraft, and PayPal credit balance, bought a new mattress, serviced and insured her car, and for a treat had some well-deserved Botox to freshen her weary late 30s face up. She had been stupid to use her own personal number as she was unable to switch it off due to her day job, friends, and family, and so her phone was on non-stop all day and night.

Despite the advert saying not a sexual service, it was a constant bombardment of confirmed appointments and then at the last minute after they had booked in and her address was given, they would ask about extras. She was so nervous that so many people knew where she lived, but in a weird way, she had this feeling that if she was attacked, then she was going to kill them.

It was almost as if the thought pumped up her adrenaline and she almost wanted something to happen, just so she could rid herself of this underlined anger and see what it was like to kill somebody and if she could get away with it. Her thoughts always spiralled out of control. She was mentally preparing for if anything was to go wrong and solely would kill in self-defence, she told herself.

She had not had any time to herself as she had been smashing it on the daily. She had not spoken with Mushy for over a month. He had lost his phone again and after 3 days of no contact with her, he had texted from his boss' phone a message to say, 'Come see me Saturday". That was it. It just was not good enough for Kim. After 4 months of her playing semi-cool, waiting for him to make his mind up about her and show her who he was truly and deeply, she decided that it was never going to happen.

She had secretly wished, prayed, and burned a torch of hope deep inside that he would stop all the nonsense and just be with her, but now with her new job, it had clearly helped him make his decision.

It was a miserable week. The full moon retrogrades had been present, winter was closing in, and Kim had caught Covid. Whilst a few days in bed feeling ill was not a big deal to Kim, the symptoms of no taste and smell were depressing. She missed the smell of her cat's fur, the fresh washing smell, and her candles; she couldn't taste or smell her coffee. She felt awful and with the intense feelings from being messed about by Mushy, she felt even worse with the rejection.

Work was becoming ever more soulless and out of her menstrual cycle, the happy days from the chart seemed to be whittling down the older she became.

Over the weeks, she turned into a total slob. Her clothes were rags with holes in and bleach stains splattered all over them. She scraped her hair back into a ponytail each day and her teeth were yellowing from too much coffee. She had not waxed her pussy, done her nails, fake tanned or shaved either. She would never be unhygienic and forced herself into the bath every night. She went into a black hole and cancelled all her massage appointments as the thought of even having to talk to anyone gave her anxiety.

She was forcing herself to eat right and she took a few walks out into the fields early morning to watch the sun come up, but still she felt nothing. She thought about a shopping trip to Zara to purchase some new clothes, but again the thought of having to attempt to put makeup on or dress decent, and see or speak to anyone including the public gave her chills down her spine. Kim knew she had down days when she was due on her period, but this was Mushy's doing.

His rejection and emotional manipulation over the months had finally taken its toll and drained the last bit of energy she had. Kim was angry at herself as she went on a bike ride, stopped at Costa, and read a book, had a spring clean, blasted her music to boost her mood, but nothing. Still, she was an empty shell. 'Ungrateful, miserable bitch,' she cursed to herself. 'You are out of debt, you work from home, you have your health, you are pretty and slim, you have nothing to be miserable about. I hate you.'

The only thing she could do was to sit tight and wait for it to hopefully pass.

Kim had not responded or reacted to Mushy's texts. She did not have the energy anymore. It must have struck a chord in him and had left him no choice but to decide because, after 4 months, he finally drove to her house and stayed the weekend. He opened his sensitive side up and pleaded for her not to hurt him and his exact words were, 'I am not going through this again, this is the last time.'

Kim thought it odd to bring such a statement to the table. It was almost like he was still in the past with an ex and Kim remembered when she had been on the second or third date and he was on the phone with his friend, he had said, 'Nah, fuck that one, I have myself better now. I have gone up, this one an 8/10,' and winked at her. Kim thought it might be a little too soon to be dating somebody who is fresh out of a relationship but she didn't ask any questions as she assumed he was single and ready to date.

Over the weekend, he was childlike, funny, and charming. Kim was laughing at his antics, and it was a warm, spiritual connection. Kim was in heaven as with the puppy he had got that she called hers and him in her home, it was like a loving little family that she had always been missing. She knew they had such a deep love and affection for each other, but her instincts were pointing her out to their huge differences.

He smoked weed constantly and she had never smoked in the house, but he was up 4-5 times a night toking on weed in bed. Kim had never let anyone smoke in the house, only out of the kitchen window. He was incredibly messy. After 10 minutes of him being in her home, there was tobacco everywhere, clothes, pots, food wrappers, wet towels, and her essential oils smell had turned into smoke.

Kim liked dinner at 5:30pm but he was busy after work doing bits and bobs, and so arrived at around 7:30pm, hence they had dinner at 8:30pm, meaning she slept badly as her body was processing huge amounts of food and sugar by the time she went to bed because he always brought lots of sweets and chocolates for after dinner, which Kim could not say no to. Kim started to smoke (out of the kitchen window of course) and over time put on a stone and a half.

Then when they were out and about Kim felt resentful because he would stop at a shop and spend up to £50 just on stupid shit like sweets, junk food, and scratch cards. He would stop at shop after shop and buy cans of JD and Lager and guzzle down a whole tin in one big gulp almost. He would also buy her tins of cocktails and so she was consuming alcohol quite a lot. They would eat out and he would order £100 worth of food and eat hardly anything.

She was looking at him throwing his money away and feeling resentful because that money could be a holiday or a road trip somewhere. But it was his money, and she forced her tidy, organised habits down and accepted that he was his own man. She argued with herself in her head that just because somebody had different habits, it didn't mean it couldn't work. They had lots of similar habits as well such as laughter, love, fitness, strength, and independence.

In fact, they were incredibly similar but so, so different in the way that they operated. Kim could not be with people for too long either and he was the same. They both needed their space to re-gather their thoughts. Mushy lived for the day and was positive, outgoing, and light-hearted as well as impulsive, greedy, and irresponsible. He had an abundance of energy, and she had an empty battery, and they seemed to balance each other out most of the time.

Kim had to cool herself off and bite her tongue as she realised she was becoming bossy and controlling, which she could not stand as she would never in a million years try to change somebody or tell somebody how to act or be.

Kim was on her way to his trailer and as she pulled up, she saw him and his boss arguing. They were both coked up seemingly. She heard Mushy shouting that his boss for the third time had not paid him again. His boss was trying to explain that if he did not get paid, then he couldn't pay him. But Mushy had to see him daily buying cocaine which probably totalled up double of what Mushy's wages were and so after the third time, Mushy had enough.

He gathered up a bunch of fireworks he had left over from 5 November, shoved them in his boss' van, threw a lit one in and closed the door. The explosions went off and the inside of his beautiful pick-up truck was black with explosion dust. Mushy came back grinning from ear to ear and his boss came running at him with a spanner and hit him over the head. 'That will do,' Mushy said laughing and got into Kim's car and tried to kiss and hug her with blood dripping down his face.

She was picking him up as he had crashed his car. He said there had been a fault on it but she knew he had probably been driving drunk and most definitely rolling a spliff with both hands whilst steering with his elbows. Her beloved puppy had been with him and he said that she had been knocked out in the crash, which made Kim seethe with anger. She had the dog stay with her more and more over the coming months.

As they drove off, Mushy shouted out the window to his boss, 'Love you, don't forget my money,' and since that day, payment was never missed again.

Kim and Mushy's bond, despite their huge differences in habits, had grown intensely strong. When she was in his arms, she felt euphoric, but when he left and went back to his own life, it gave her time to think things to death. She was in love but at what cost to her fundamental being? She had put on 2 stone in weight, her skin was incredibly bad, and she was smoking and drinking, not sleeping and not exercising. She was becoming insecure and unconfident, and they were the worst traits in herself or in anybody else that she disliked.

She compromised it due to her spiritual love needs being met but in that, she had lost herself by becoming his bad habits. She had been slowly trying to introduce him to her world of adventure and escapism, but it was always ruined by his inability to give quality time away. She had booked Tattershall Lakes for them both, which was a static caravan with a hot tub.

Due to him working and doing his "bits and bats", they made their way up there at 4:30pm on Friday and on the whole day Saturday, he had to drive back to work in Leicester, which had already been agreed as it only takes 1 hour and a half to drive. So she knew he finished work on Saturdays at around 13:00 but he left her there all day and arrived back at 9pm drunk and ready to go out for food.

After food and a very long ass day of Kim brewing up feelings of huge disappointment and feeling like an idiot, the last thing on her mind was sex. Of course, they tried and it was just impossible for Kim to connect to him after her expectation of a romantic weekend had been smashed to pieces, and once again the awkward, acrobatic, sex began. She swallowed her feelings up and didn't respond, react, or vocalise her disappointment.

It was New Year's Eve and Kim had booked a nice hotel for them with a spa. She would have loved to have set off in the afternoon and have a nice meal, followed by a steam room and jacuzzi with him to relax in the hotel room and have incredible sex all refreshed and glowing and healthy. Mushy said he had to finish work at 4pm, which she found unbelievable as his boss had a family and would surely be doing something, but that is what he told her so she should not question it.

As she was driving at 5pm to go and pick him up, he texted her to say that his nephew was having a bit of trouble and was coming to stay and work with him and was on his way to Leicester. "Listen, he is near Leicester, come and pick me up from the pub and we can go from there. He should be here by the time you get here. Can you go pick me a weed up to save time", he texted.

The weed stop was on the way to him, so it was not a problem. She drove up the estate with a trainer hanging from a lamppost and to the house with loads of youths outside with their man mags and caps on. Kim knew to knock on the door, and she knew of the woman previously just from being in Mushy's passenger seat. The house was a typical occurrence from her old estate. Kids everywhere, dogs everywhere, teenagers hanging about.

Back in the day, there was always a house like this where everyone would hang around. The woman opened the door and Kim asked if she could get a £50 for Mushy. The woman looked a bit miffed but let her in nevertheless. Kim understood that it was stupid for Mushy to send Kim around in the woman's eyes as Kim could have been anybody really. The woman was your typical estate woman, no fucks given, loud, overconfident, and was herself with anyone and everyone. Just Kim's type.

Hard but friendly and salt of the earth people. Kim often wondered why she had the same upbringing as all these types of people, on the same estates, with the same benefits, the same poverty and yet, she was a totally different kettle of fish. She got the weed and drove to the pub where hopefully Mushy was. "Pick me up a few JDS and Coke Tins, love", he texted. No problem.

At least that meant he may be ready to set off as it is now 6:30pm and it would take another hour or so drive to get to the hotel. Kim arrived at the pub and Mushy was in his full element, having a game of pool with a full, fresh pint of lager in no way ready to go. 'I'm just having this pint and we'll set off, baby. This is my nephew, little legs we call him.' Kim sat down with him; he looked all but 15 years old. She delved as to why he was in Leicester, and he revealed he was on the run.

He said he had been in Scotland and didn't like it, and had run from a boarding house or some sort of accommodation. He was sweet and Kim had actually felt bad that he was staying with Mushy because how would he cope with no hot water, no toilet, shitting in a bucket. There was no electricity and so it was freezing, and he would have to keep the petrol topped up in order to put the gas on the cooker rings for heat. He would not be able to charge his phone or have WI-FI.

She didn't think a 15-year-old would like that, but he assured Kim he just wanted to get his head down as she was contemplating offering for him to go to her house but decided not to get involved. Mushy ordered yet another round of drinks and by this time, Kim was deflated and sipped on the JD & Coke that she did not even want. They were supposed to be in a hotel by now fresh and relaxed from the steam room and enjoying each other's bodies, but here she was, yet again.

He did have emotional intelligence and when he saw her face and slugged shoulders, ushered them to go. He had to drop Carl at the trailer first, which was 5 minutes away, and as they pulled up to the park, Mushy missed the usual entrance and started to go the back way around where there is a field and a fence that you have to climb through to get to the back way of his trailer. Kim already knew why he was going this way—it was an impression that he wanted to give to Carl about how remote he was going to be from now on.

So instead of pulling up on the gravel and walking 2ft to the trailer, he made his way over the muddy field. As soon as they had gotten onto the mud, they halted to a stop. It was pitch-black and it had been raining, and now the car was stuck in sludge and the more he revved, the deeper the wheels sunk in. Both Mushy and Carl tirelessly tried to free the car with pieces of wood and pushing whilst Kim was instructed to accelerate. After 20 minutes, Mushy and Carl were covered from head to toe in mud.

Kim had no doubt that Mushy would solve the problem as he was a real man that way but why oh why did he not be normal and go his usual way? As they drove away from the pitch-black trailer leaving Carl to enjoy his downtime, it was 19:45. A pit stop at the Garage for him to roll a spliff and down a few tins more of JD, they were finally on their way until Mushy announced he had left his phone in the pub on charge and so back they went to the pub, and finally, they were on the way.

Kim had booked dinner for 8pm and so she re-arranged for 21:30 but did not even want to go at this point. She had been really looking forward to this but just like Tattersall, it seemed like he was emotionally unavailable and avoidant when it came to quality time. They arrived at the restaurant, and it would have been wonderful as it was Thai and Indian, both of their favourite dishes in one place, but she was so tired and she had not eaten as she knew she was having dinner, but now it had passed, just like the excitement had passed.

Every time they had come to an Indian restaurant, Mushy always asked for "big crisps" meaning poppadoms and it then took a further 5 minutes for the waiters to figure out from his hand gestures that he meant poppadoms. Now as Kim had witnessed this many times, she pondered why he didn't just say poppadoms, but this was his 'thing'. The waiter luckily knew in seconds that he meant poppadoms and from Mushy's face, the waiter's quick no nonsense response seemed to have burst his fun.

But that didn't stop him and so he went on to order not what was on the menu, but asking if he could mix this with that and that with this, until there were 3 waiters around the table trying to figure out from his ever more confusing demands what he actually wanted to order. She prayed that they got it right, otherwise he would kick off. As usual, he ordered £100 worth and ate only a small percentage, but again it was his money.

Kim was vexed at this point, but she was also angry at herself again for being annoyed at somebody for being themselves. It would not have been so bad if she had some energy but she felt it was an onslaught at this point. They got back to the hotel and Kim felt like some weird, wired zombie. It was almost as if her whole body had gone into flight mode and shut down as the whole afternoon had been a 100mph. They lay on the bed and the sex was excruciating.

It was the most awkward Kim had ever felt. She was as stiff as a bored and had zoomed out of the experience. Mushy was as stated before very emotionally intelligent and he obviously thought she was a weirdo. She explained that she was tired and on an empty battery, but as he did not get an empty battery, he would never understand. Especially with sex. The disappointment was so rife.

Kim had hoped to have a beautiful spa day and a meal, and then to be in the bathroom mirror watching themselves or bent over the dressing table in sexy underwear making love that led up to filth, and then fall back on the bed and spend the rest of the evening laughing and messing about; but no, each planned event that was supposed to be about quality and relaxing, and a destress from her already miserable, stressed life, turned out to be manic and her battery did not have anything left.

It was becoming excruciating and probably excruciating for him too as he had tonnes of energy and whirl-winded himself through the day. When she finally did break through his barrier and get him to relax, it was a beautiful thing and there were beautiful moments where she could see his soul, but the effort spent getting to this was taking her life.

The next morning was better and after a swim and steam room on her own as he went to the gym, they headed for breakfast. As she was rested and relaxed, her annoyance at him had disappeared and yet again, she was mesmerised by his charm and his dreamy, light blue eyes, and chose to ignore him phlegm-ing his greenies on the floor, throwing his JD cans out of the car window, and all the other qualities that made her shudder.

The love she had for him far outweighed the negative aspects and Kim was adamant it was a Ying and Yang connection rather than the opposing magnets that her gut was telling her.

Knock, knock, knock. Knock, knock, knock. It continued until Kim stirred in the realisation that it was not a dream. She looked at the time and it was 3:30am. Fuck, it is Lee, she thought. She popped her head out of the window and panicked because she and Mushy were in deep now and there was no way she could see Lee even in a friendship way as she would not disrespect the man she loved so deeply like that.

It was two police officers and she asked what on earth was going on and they asked if she knew anybody by the name of

Carl. At first, she did not recall. She was truthful and she did not know a Carl but then it dawned on her, Mushy's nephew, Carl. 'Does your telephone number end 366?' One of the officers asked.

'Yes, I think so,' she replied. Kim went downstairs and let them in at their request. Kim had texted Carl on the way to the hotel to ask if he was ok and so for some reason, he was on the run or a young person at risk, his phone had been intervened and her number had come up. They searched her house and Kim's heart was pounding from her chest—not for Carl but there was no way she could mention Mushy or give them any idea where he lived.

Mushy was probably wanted and Carl could lead them right to her Mushy. She was a terrible liar and tried her best to stay calm and think of a story. The policeman was watching her every facial expression and he was not an idiot, he deals with liars every day. A lightbulb moment came into Kim's head, and she remembered that incidents previously to do with Lee would be logged to her address. One was when he stole a SIM card that was included in her internet package and racked up huge bills by going over the data allowance.

She had clicked it was him after ringing the internet company and they had said somebody in London was using the SIM card. They then cancelled the SIM card and were supposed to send her a new number, but instead sent her the SIM card with the same number attached, so Kim was receiving an influx of calls from drug dealers day and night thinking that it was Lee.

As Kim was telling a real story but applying it to a different situation, her body language relaxed and she explained that this Carl may have been given the number in pursuit of drugs or God knows what, but it had nothing to do with her. The officers were happy with the story as everything made sense and the incidents were filed at her address. She knew Mushy needed to change his number and advised him to do so the next day.

Mushy was sorry that something had involved Kim and that week as he had Carl to impress, he was distant and unavailable yet again. He probably could have sensed Kim pulling back in order to recharge and his passion for her had been killed off by the awkward sexual experiences and the growing realisation of the butterflies wearing off, revealing their incompatibility furthermore. Kim felt sad that the excitement and adventure of getting to know each other was seemingly coming to an end.

The realisation that she was involved with yet another man child that was wild and free and destined for death or prison instead of her dream of a man to make her safe and look after her was a sad thought.

Kim had been paid on 31 December and her balance was already -£200. Her Car Tax of £360 and MOT of £50 were due that month. She could only get her Car Tax if she passed her MOT which seemed unlikely due to the electrics beginning to fade, a brake fault, doors would not lock, the driver side door would not shut properly, and only one key would now start the engine as her spare key would not work despite several attempts to change the battery.

Mushy said he could get somebody to put the MOT through and then pay for anything that needed fixing. He also kept saying he would buy her a car after Christmas. He had said this quite a few times now and the more he said it and it didn't happen, the more disappointed she became. It was not his responsibility to buy her a car, but again, the want deep inside her for a man to show that he loves her and wants to look after her was being awoken, and then crushed due to nothing of the sort ever occurring.

He then again would mention both getting a car, but again she stone-walled that idea as she did not trust him—number one his driving and number two, he had smashed his ex's car up.

The threat to Kim's peace was becoming a regular occurrence; she started to panic as she thought of life lying to the police and the instability of it all. She thought maybe to SORN her car and then as he had crashed his car previously, none of them would be driving and wouldn't be able to see each other as he lived an hour away with no other transport option available than driving. It was a beautiful bond she had with him and it had laughter and love and affection, but was it worth this feeling?

That week, he hadn't seemed very interested in her and she knew why. Her disapproval of him had seeped through her and attached itself to her body language no matter how much she had tried to disguise it. She knew he was feeling rejected by her, she had seen it in his eyes, and she felt bad as she knew of all people what it was like to have people not like your character when you were only being your true self.

The messages had been bland all week but then he messaged and asked if his daughter could come and stay the weekend at her house. Kim said yes as she admired it when he had made an effort to see his daughter. She pondered on why he did not see his youngest and she really felt for the mother of his children, as he seemed "super dad" to the children due to certain situations.

For example, at Christmas, he would give them £500 each and stated, 'I will give my daughters anything they want.' Kim's eyes went off into the distance when he would say things like this, as she thought, Well, what about the mother coping on all on her own with no financial help? He did not pay any maintenance or child support. It was £200 dropped here and there, which did not cover even a few weeks' food shop. His daughter stayed for the weekend.

Mushy worked all weekend and arrived back at 8pm each night leaving only an hour to have with his daughter. His daughter had freely spoken to Kim about all the previous women in his life—one after the other after the other. There was a lot of talk about violence and how a few of his exes were crackheads and how he had been violent to a lot of women. It was almost like a warning and the casual way his daughter rolled it off her tongue to let Kim know exactly what she was dealing with.

But then Kim also had to judge him on what she knew of him and she could never imagine him being violent with her, but they both didn't argue with each other either, so there was never an opportunity for him to lose his temper in order to find out. Their styles were almost the same, stubborn, stonewalling, and non-confrontational when it came to emotional issues as much as the ongoing differences were obvious, so were their similarities and neither of them was into drama.

Kim, who was watching his interactions like a hawk, could see that he just could not relate to females. She could see that he had a huge uncomfortable attitude towards getting too close to women. There was a huge wall with him and he avoided getting emotionally close to any female, even his own daughters. The only woman he was obsessed with was his birth mother with whom seemingly he was desperate to create in her a need for him.

He constantly fuelled her with lager and weed. It was either him desperate for acceptance or that or they were both co-dependents accepting and normalising each other's addictions as they were both clearly alcoholics. Kim could see in Mushy the obvious addiction gene that had been passed down from his mother to him and his brother. By now his brother's face was so puffy, it almost looked like it would pop if you poked it.

There were other siblings too that Mushy had mentioned and were all addicts. She had seen Mushy go up and down a little bit, but over the short time they had been together, she almost believed that he had it under control but knew that was just another red flag that she was pushing down to the bottom of her gut.

Friday morning, Kim awoke to her beautiful man. He was always no matter what on form at 6am with his workout. She was so puzzled at how big and ripped he was as he downed cans of JD and Coke and lager all day long. He ate terribly, gorging on takeaway fast food every night unless they were cooking at her and due to his weed habit, he would spend £10-£15 every night on goodies. Crisps, chocolate, biscuits, and cans of pop.

She was bemused at how he had the energy to get up as fresh as a daisy and work out, as she had never seen him eat anything nutritious and he barely drank water. She wondered sometimes also with the sex, how he kept such stamina. As much as she hated the acrobatic sex, she knew he was a good fuck and sometimes she thought he may have a heart attack as he was pounding her like his life depended on it. She didn't know how he did it. How did he have such stamina, even though he had COPD and never had a spliff out of his mouth?

It was almost as if a drag from a spliff was some form of fresh air for him. She always felt stupid when she rode him (which was a rarity these days as she was too conscious of her ageing body or too pent-up with stress in order to let go) as she would be out of breath in seconds. She hated it as she knew she could orgasm so easily but his determination to make her have an orgasm and the pent-up stress from the day and work put an overwhelming pressure on her and she just couldn't let go.

He and their dog (that he had purchased immediately after she said she would love a dog) had been at Kim's all week. She was surprised at how much she had enjoyed it. She loved their puppy. It was an XL bulldog which was trending with chavs and horrid breeders at the time. But "Aggie", although all muscle and pit bull looking, was the most beautiful, softest dog and she loved that dog like it was a child.

She despised that Mushy said he was going to take her to have her ears cropped and luckily, he did not go through with it, which pleased Kim as she knew he was compassionate deep down and that is what she loved about him the most. Underneath his strength, there was a beautiful soul and she so wished that the few times she had managed to connect with that soul would be a more regular occurrence. She loved having Aggie, the cats and Mushy at home for that week.

It was as if she had all the love, and she could love and nurture in return, which is what she had longed and craved for so long. She had not minded the tobacco everywhere, the wet towels, the dishes, and the smell of potent weed in place of her usual essential oils. She loved him going to work and cooking for him when he arrived home; it didn't matter that it was 7pm or 8pm as he was with her, and he seemed to realise that he actually liked this setup and spoke words of buying them a nice trailer on a site somewhere.

Kim was excited at the thought, excited that he finally understood she wasn't a woman who was going to tag him down, message him about his whereabouts, and bug him to spend time with her. She understood he was wild and free, and he had an insatiable amount of energy that he needed to get rid of by dashing around and keeping busy from his torturous thoughts; he was never going to be a pipe and slippers man.

But all she had wanted him to do was the manly thing and make sure she was ok with somewhere to live, and she would be excruciatingly happy in a domestic role and having nothing to do with the outside world. This is where their yin and yang could work. She knew who he was and what he was about and if only he would stop being scared and did that one thing for her, then he could get on with his busy doing nothing life and have a distressed woman at home ready to serve him his food and suck his cock with pleasure.

Mushy was on the list to get a house and he had spoken about this numerous times to her but never mentioned the house as a way for them to be together so that she would be looked after; he mentioned it solely to put a grow on in there and make a profit. Kim's alarm bells had always rang when he mentioned it and she changed the conversation sharpish as it was just another lightbulb to disturb her peace.

It made her think of being stuck in a house with a grow on worrying about being robbed at knifepoint as he had a mouth like a woman sometimes and couldn't help but impress people with his tales, which wasn't the most intelligent move to be telling every Tom, Dick and Harry what your business is, but that was Mushy all over. Ever the charmer, the show-off, the man about town. In his childlike charm, he didn't realise that people were bitter.

People loved him but they also despised themselves and their own shit lives, and as much as people seemed nice and trustworthy, the majority were watching him and waiting for his optimistic and overconfident personality to be squashed so they could feel that their own shit lives were ok.

Payday came around again, and Kim was skint as she hadn't been too keen on the perves that were coming through her door. She had never remotely said or acted in a sexual way, but she knew why they came for a massage from her. In their own minds, they were fantasising about her, fantasising that one day they might just be able to attract her attention or get her out for a meal. It was the chase, you see. Men loved the unattainable.

She admired men's efforts and pitied them at the same time. It was a man's instinct to chase and conquer at any cost to their ego. Kim by no means was Jennifer Lopez but in comparison to the men coming through her door, she was a cut above the rest in their eyes. Kim was only trying to earn a few quid as easily as possible, but the ever-growing pressure of her clients' subconscious thoughts was putting pressure on her. She found it vile that they wanted her.

She did not want them to look at her in that way but knew that was the deal. Her last client had messaged her to advise if it was ok to have a massage if he had a wax booked in the morning. Kim replied to him that it would be silly to have a massage after a wax as it would be sore, and he said he would cancel the wax and still come for a massage. He arrived and everything was as normal.

As she stuck her knuckles in the bottom of his back, he started to arch his back and stick his bum in the air almost trying to get in a doggy-style position. Kim's rage boiled up. Number one because of his sheer cheek of trying to turn this into something it would never be, but mainly at the repulsion of a grown man trying to be feminine and putting himself in a doggy-style position like some little bitch. It repulsed her to see a man like that acting like some submissive woman.

She pulled her anger together and firmly but kindly worded that he needed to keep still and relax, otherwise his muscles would stay tense. He got the message as she firmly pushed his back down onto the massage bed and carried on as normal. As she was kneading his back in the last 10 minutes, she noticed that his back only had a few blonde baby hairs and she asked him why he was going to have his back waxed. He replied, 'No, not my back. I have my balls and sack waxed.'

The rage in her once again arose. Upon placing the advert, it had stated NOT A SEXUAL SERVICE in capital letters. He had been a regular client and so he knew it was NOT A SEXUAL SERVICE. She knew logically that men would not understand that and would die trying, but her own personal issues of not being heard ever by anyone enraged her. She wanted the power of Mushy, she wanted people to look at her and know not to mess with her or say anything untoward.

But she was a walkover. Only people like Mushy had that special charm. After this, she had cancelled all her appointments for the month and now it was payday yet again and she was back in the same position as before. She started to feel resentment again towards Mushy for her having to struggle. What man would let his Mrs go through this if he loved her? He obviously didn't. Her own existence doomed her yet again. "Working" which she hated and having to work another job massaging desperate cunts just so she could afford to eat and run a car.

She still hadn't managed to buy any clothes for herself or go on any holidays or even a weekend away, and Mushy's £10 notes here or there were not helping. He always told her 'Book it and I will pay for it when we get there.' But he didn't understand or listen when she said she didn't have the money in the first instance to pay for both of them to secure a booking to do anything leisurely. She was even more insulted by the fact that these men thought she would miraculously turn into brass at their £50 offerings for "stress relief", the fucking cheek of it.

If she did, she would at least charge £500 and afford herself a holiday. She was gaining a newfound respect for brasses. How they could fuck these men were beyond belief. She herself would be homeless than do that to herself. But she respected the women who had no feelings or at best could cut their emotions off for 2 minutes to suck a dick. At least they were rolling in it, financially secure, and non-reliant on no fucker.

Over the coming months, Mushy showed her time and time again how much of a real man he was, and this made Kim even more determined to make him commit to her. He would always run her a bath and fill the bathroom with candles, make her a coffee in the morning how she liked it, brought her flowers, and he was still mentioning the trailer and Kim went along with the idea waiting for it to unfold. By now, she had taken on his habits and she had lost herself.

She had put on weight and she was smoking and drinking more casually than ever before. She had no self-esteem and the sex was suffering because of it. She felt as if she had lost control over her well-being, and it wasn't his fault. She could have some self-control but it was near enough impossible to say no to these things. Kim's motto was "out of sight, out of mind" but when chocolate, tobacco, and alcohol were in front of her, she had no control to refuse.

She reflected that she wanted to be a housewife as to be healthy and glowing and be the best she could be, not a chubby, yellow-toothed, G&T Tin drinker with bad skin.

Mushy was really getting along with Kim's dad. Her dad was a character all in his own right. He was all but 5'3 in height, 72 years of age, covered head to toe in red Indian-themed tattoos, and spawned a different coloured Mohican every week. He also smoked weed and dabbled in mind-altering drugs on occasion.

She would watch him whilst he was on another planet listening to Pink Floyd, dancing around the garden clearly admiring all the flowers and trees he had grown, now seemingly coming to life in front of his very eyes. Kim had loved living with her dad but his constant partying and loud music disturbed her peace greatly. Kim wasn't a music person at all. She blamed that on her dad as he had tortured her with the likes of the Beatles and Fleetwood Mac as a child and she felt sure it had turned her into the noise-hating person she was today.

Her mum had been somewhat of a hippie back in the day, walking the kids around the block barefoot in a kaftan. Her mum had been a beautiful woman. Dark olive skin, piercing bright blue/grey eyes, and a strong jawline with sucked-in cheeks like a supermodel. Her dad also had beautiful grey eyes and was dark olive-skinned with a killer cheekbone structure.

They made a good-looking couple and were social butterflies, loving to throw parties every weekend, inviting all and sundry to their house where her dad had built a bar in the living room and a room to host parties, that included a pool table, darts board, karaoke machine, and disco lights. Their 3-storey council house was huge and it was a happy upbringing despite the extreme lack of money, they were like everyone else on the estate, so Kim and her brother didn't know any different.

Despite the games room with the items paid for on credit, they were poor but happy and did not go without. They were happy with their ice-cream sodas, lollies made with orange cordial in a mug and a fork stuck in it for the handle, and a good old game of British bulldog, Kirby, and a complimentary holiday to Mablethorpe. It was obvious to Kim as to why she had such an interest in wild souls and feral people. Her mum and dad were not the norm.

They were interesting characters different from all the other parents or families she knew, and she had inherited at least that from them and blessed them for it as she would never want to fit into the bland society; the middle class with their boring conversations and conformant ways, their boring dress sense, and mundane ways. Even though as a kid she had screamed and begged the words daily "Why can't we be normal?", "Why can't we be a normal family?", but now more than ever she appreciated that she hadn't come from the norm.

It was boring and had made her live her life fully all the way up until now. She had travelled the world, learned another language, been a lap dancer, and never had to conform or settle down. If she became bored, she would pack a suitcase and go to another county the next day. But now all that was behind her because she was too old to dance in her head and so now, she was stuck in society, in a job, wasting her days in front of a computer like a zombie that she had sworn she would never become.

Now her hopes for escapism were hopefully in Mushy taking ownership of her so she didn't have to anymore.

Mushy always had sorted her dad out with weed for free, even though her dad only smoked lightly at the weekends, and had offered him money constantly for it. Mushy insisted he was family now and family sorted out family. Kim was like her dad. Suspicious, didn't want anyone to have a hold over them for love or money. They both knew to be independent and not have the chance for anyone to throw anything in their faces.

But Kim knew Mushy was a generous soul and hated it sometimes that he seemed to give all of his money away and even hated the fact that he brought her flowers and chocolates when she could have done with the £15 towards a bill.

She arrived at her dad's on Saturday and Mushy had arranged to come for a drink after work. He was doing security for the small bollocks fox hunting lot. She knew not to speak of it as Mushy was just in it for the money, but the brutality from him against the protesters was what she hated. She had seen videos of Mushy's balaclava face and being a bully boy to what she deemed as heroes. Anyone sticking up for animals was a person to be celebrated in her mind, not to have the living shit kicked out of them.

However, she also knew sickly that this was why she found him so attractive. She knew he was capable of violence and it pricked her internal instincts for a real man. She would prefer him as a monster who could control his violence though. That would have been the better goal for her. Her dad's girlfriend of 9 years was there. Bat shit crazy she was but Kim, despite being riled at the constant chatter or utter shit, really liked her. She was off the wall, heart of gold but her weakness was what Kim disliked in her.

She was a victim of some sort of abuse in her past and suffered severely from PTSD. If you could get her on a good day, she was gold, but on her regular mental health days, she was a nightmare in the making. Kim had compassion for anyone in bad times, as "we all have them" she would say, but she was a great believer in strength, overcoming, being sturdy, and dealing with your shit. She had a resemblance in traits to her own mother.

She let her emotions overrun and torture her mind until their eyes were glazed over and they were lost in the abyss. Both of them had done stretches in mental hospitals and this time around, it wasn't her dad's fault. Either way, his Mrs was having a good day and they shared a game of cards and started on a few cans. Kim nor her dad was really feeling it; it was an almost gloomy atmosphere. It got later and later and seemed as though Mushy had planned this; he was making excuses about when he was arriving.

It was 7pm and usually, the Saturday drinks started at 3pm. He walked through the doorway nearly filling it and half having to bend down to get through. Looking at him next to her dad and his partner who was also all but 5'3, he looked huge. He was huge. His face was like thunder and everyone in the room felt his dark presence. It was uncomfortable as the air filled with the aggression radiating from his face. He sat down and rolled a ridiculously double-joined spliff which was unnecessary and OTT as he never usually did this.

He was on edge and fidgeting and riling off into conversation with himself about Grime music and the hood. Kim had a stone wall, dismissive face; she would never hide her distaste for something. Kim could never hide her body language or resting bitch face. It was more uncomfortable as her dad was old school. He was from a day of respect, where the men wore suits and respected each other. It was a different sort of gang back in the day.

Mushy's real dad was exactly the same as her dad, from the photos she had seen of him, and the stories told of him. Both Mushy's dad and her own would have agreed on how much they hated youths of today, with their stupid ghetto talk and Gucci man bags, listening to Grime music and the fake troubles of growing up in a council estate. Kim interjected him as he was going on, almost ranting to himself frantically about how she didn't know what real life was and she wasn't from the hood.

She cringed with embarrassment but argued her case that she was from a council estate and it had never bothered her. She said that she had been happy and they knew not of hard times as even in the poorest of England on the poorest of council estates, you still had benefits—food, housing, medical care, and schooling.

She also couldn't help but point out the fact that he had been adopted at the age of 4 into a middle-class family, in a brought house, with whom his adoptive father had his own business and they had not wanted for anything. She knew plenty of lads like him from the suburbs who loved the idea of being from a rough area and did all they could to appear like the main man from the hood.

She knew Mushy had returned to Leicester at around 15 to be reunited with his real family, who were by all accounts the same as the family from the TV programme Shameless, but she was enraged. As rough as he was and however much he had entangled himself with the most common of England, he sure as hell didn't have the same upbringing as "us".

As she viciously spurted out her last fact, and only at that fact did her dad say the words, 'Yeah, that's right,' only meaning to say he agreed about her upbringing, Mushy had jumped the fucking roof. It was as if he had some sort of thought for all but one second as to not aim his anger at Kim, as she was so logical and factual that he could not handle her response, so he jumped up and started to shout at her dad viciously and completely went on one about how much of a piss taker her dad was, how he always gave him weed and this is how he gets treated.

It was a complete shock to all in the room and everybody was scared at the level of anger that had arisen in Mushy. Kim was screaming inside as she saw her dad freeze in fear and look at the floor, retreating into a fearful shell. Mushy was carrying on his attack squaring up to her dad. There it was again, that bully side, the uncontrollable violence, and at what? A little old man who was high as a kite and said all but two words at the wrong time.

He grabbed Aggie by the scruff of the neck and sped away in his car. It was the most erratic she had ever seen him and the stories his daughter had told her previously were starting to come to light. Kim knew the line had been crossed. Lee had robbed her dad and caused all manner of shit. Her dad had always forgiven Lee and shook his hand and welcomed him back into the home, only for Lee to return the favour by robbing anything that he could get his hands on in the house. She wasn't going to let anyone disrespect her family ever again.

Weeks had passed and Kim was shocked at herself as she had cried all but once and that was only over not being able to see Aggie anymore. There were no tears for him, no moments of despair and nothing in the resemblance of how a breakup would feel to somebody. She finally received a message from him and from there, it turned into a battle of who was right about what events had occurred that night.

She found herself bargaining again, bargaining by saying that all he had to do was make it right with her dad and all would be well. Her dad wasn't even bothered about the event and Kim started to think things through and remembered the spat that she had previously with a girlfriend that resulted in Kim dragging her dad's bird out of their bed naked after a dreadful night of one of her dad's birds meltdowns.

Kim immediately felt terrible and did everything she could to assure her that it was a moment of madness after a 15-hour shift and a sleep-in at the nut house that she worked in, she had just lost her shit being sleep deprived and it was just bad timing. They both had been shit that night and had moved on very quickly indeed, much to Kim's relief, as she had felt horrible, and she did really like the woman.

Mushy drove round to her father's house and apologised in the way of giving him a meaningful handshake and some weed, which dad understandably felt uncomfortable taking from him now, but Mushy being Mushy, again would not have any of it and insisted he have it. Kim felt a pang of relief in her bones. She knew how stubborn Mushy was and she knew that he still felt that he had been attacked and he had done no wrong, but neither the less, his resolve with her father had put things right in her mind.

For Mushy to do it was, in her head, an admirable action, probably due to the fact that how many times Lee had said sorry and promised that he would right his wrongs towards her family and had never once kept that word and just continued more wrongs.

Kim and Mushy went to grab a Turkish takeaway. Kim waited in the car and she gushed at watching her man walk past and everyone staring at him like some sort of fucking God. As he neared the shop, he stopped to talk to a woman who had her small child with her. Kim's back went up immediately as the conversation seemed awkward between them. It looked like an awkward romantic encounter to her, like it was his ex or something as their body language was extremely uncomfortable.

She was all head down and stiff and he was jumping about like he had hot rocks near his bollocks. What Kim didn't like was how he was acting. He was being charming, keeping the conversation going, doing his smile, and engaging her with his charm. He had widened his sparkly eyes and was smiling, flirting. Kim knew this was more than just bumping into someone, but then was she just feeling threatened, he was like this with everyone no?

Kim was fixated on their encounter and the woman made her way to the bus stop as Mushy entered the shop to get food. As he came out, he ran over the road to the bus stop and as ever, gave the boy a bag of sweets and gave her a £20 note.

This was not unusual, this was Mushy all over, but something didn't sit right in Kim's stomach. As he got into the car, Kim immediately asked who it was. He replied casually that it was a friend of his mum's who had been up the trailer having a drink one time.

Kim accepted the answer as they had just gotten over the incident with her father and she didn't want to ruin anything further, but men were fucking stupid. They lied not realising that women were natural fucking detectives by nature. The logic of Kim immediately came into force. The facts kicked in that this woman was at a fucking bus stop and clearly lived in Beaumont Leys, the same as her and his mum's trailer had been moved next to his trailer (that was miles away and an hour's drive at the least in the middle of nowhere) only a few months back.

How the fuck would this woman have got to the trailer unless it was a lift from him. Kim's head was racing and her heart nearly left her chest. She was so uncomfortable as she could smell bullshit. She had always trusted Mushy; he was the one man whom she could look in the eyes and feel trust, and that is what had endeared her and made her feel at least somewhat safe in that respect. She was so, so disappointed and she didn't know how she was going to handle this as there was something not right about it. She knew from his body language, he was fucking lying.

She sat with the thoughts of the interaction between Mushy and that woman for weeks. She never said anything and she tried her mightiest to push the feelings down. She didn't want to ruin what she and Mushy had but she had to find out the truth. The visions of them haunted her, but what she was most angry about was how he had acted right in front of Kim's face.

If Kim had have seen her ex or an encounter at the shop and Mushy was there, she would have either flat out ignored him or at the very least said, 'Hi, you ok?' and walked off. She imagined what Mushy would have done if he had to watch Kim bashing her eyelids and stroking her hair, giggling away with some man right in front of his fucking face. He would have murdered them both in cold blood. It only proved to Kim that he had no fear of losing Kim or no value to her.

Not even hiding his amor for this other woman and carrying on right in front of Kim's eyes. The worst thing was Kim now bumped into this woman a lot. She had cycled past her once and belled her out of the way, and as the woman turned around, Kim had recognised her. Kim was dying to stop and interrogate her on how she knew Mushy, but it just seemed erratic and crazy to do at the time. The impact it had on Kim over the weeks had hit her badly.

He would tell her how beautiful she was, but all Kim could think about was if he had cheated on her. She reverted back to her old ways of how she was with Lee and the emotional pain of somebody hurting her heart so brutally. Cheating was such a brutal thing to her; it was the sin of all sins in her mind. She was as loyal as a fucking dog and she would never want to put somebody through that pain, and so she couldn't comprehend that Mushy could put her through that and break her heart.

Nothing was factual but women's instincts were always right.

It was Bank Holiday weekend and she had booked 4 days off. Mushy had pulled away from her and instead of giving him space, she was enraged. He can't keep pulling away and being distant and then coming back when he felt like it, she seethed in her head. He had swerved her on offering to do something for the weekend and said he had a job doing security on the doors at some pub.

She didn't say a word but the jealousy and rage rose in her soul thinking of a busy Bank Holiday with all the drunk females swooning over him. It was enough to make bile come up from her stomach and hit her throat. He had lost his phone and weirdly for once, he had written his new number down on a rizla for her to have, but she had lost it understandably. A rizla wasn't the easiest of things to look after. Kim knew that he had her number, but yet again, she heard nothing from him.

It was a Sunday, and she needed a drink. The sun was out, and she was sick of the emotional turmoil she had let enter her peaceful life. She dolled herself up the best she could and headed into town to meet Zack. She loved the shit hole pubs, the spit and sawdust places, where nobody gave a fuck about what anybody looked like, and Kim loved the weirdos and characters that frequented them. The Market Tavern was her go. It was cheap and rough as arseholes.

She had not been here for a long time though and as the shots went down, she knew she had gotten over all this shit a long time ago. It was the same old shit for herself; she would get drunk, go off her fucking rocker, order cocaine, and regret it forever. She had a good time for a few hours but knew herself so well by now, to listen to the warning light in her head when dealers were near her, and Zack was already halfway in the toilet.

She slipped out of the pub and ran to a street food café, sat down and ordered a burrito. She nearly cried into her burrito and sat there all alone whilst Mushy was no doubt putting his charm offensive on the wide choice of pussy that would be swooning around him this very moment with not a care for her in his head.

The next day, she was pleased she had eaten and hadn't succumbed to going past the line she used to cross when her old voice in her head used to say to her "fuck it". She sat on the sofa with a latte and in boredom, re-activated her Facebook to have a nose at people posting utter shit. Immediately, a "people you may know" suggestion came up of "Sharlene Ball". She recognised the woman. It was the woman from the shop.

The woman from the interaction that had ensured the demise of her and Mushy as nothing had been right since that day. Kim had made sure of that one. She instinctively knew that a few clicks more in the next few seconds were going to secure her already secured suspicions, and she groaned in pain and pondered on whether it was worth doing it to herself. Number one, women made themselves look like fucking Angelina Jolie in pictures and even though it was fake and edited, it still had the power to make women feel like a piece of shit in their own skin.

Kim tapped on the first profile picture and instinctively looked at the people who had liked the picture looking for any hearts. There it was immediately. The first like of the stupid pouting, edited picture. First fucking picture as well. The rest were on private, but no doubt he was there, stroking another woman's fucking ego. She looked at the date, 18 February 2021.

She looked at the Valentine's Day card still sitting on her table, full of beautiful words about his love for Kim and all the things he loved about her. She remembered he had put rose petals all over her bed in a heart shape and worded petals out to say, "I love you". And for what? For him to be yet again reaching out to this woman. She couldn't stand it when people said, "It's only a like". Well, ok. Why didn't he like the Christmas picture or the family picture then?

Why like the sexual ones? She didn't even have his number to go off on him and all she wanted at that moment was to let that swarmy cunt know that she knew. She never doubted herself once. She knew there was no evidence but she wasn't one of them birds who was crazy. She had never bugged him about other women; she was never jealous as she was confident in herself and found it unattractive to go on like that. But from that moment at the shops, she had known. It isn't called gut instinct for no reason.

He texted her the next morning after 4 days of silence to say, "Morning, why have you not messaged me". Kim was glad she wasn't in sight of him because her head had gone. Her body was shaking with rage from head to toe. She had rung him immediately, but as soon as her venom hit him in explaining that she knew who Sharlene was and he hung up on her. He told her to fuck off on a message and said for her to block him. It told Kim yet again everything she needed to know and she hated herself for ever setting eyes on him.

The next few weeks were torturous but fruitful. Not only had she been proven right, but the fact she had wasted a whole year believing this man loved her in his own way. She felt the worst thing she could feel, humiliation. She decided she was going to take this pain and challenge it. She wasn't going to sit there like a muppet for some cunt who didn't value her.

She booked a week off annual leave and went deep down into the battlefield of the mind.

She was fucking nuts. She felt like Bear Grylls in some sort of war zone in her mind. She isolated herself from the world and sat with the excruciating pain day and night with no distractions, hell-bent on a fight with it. She only ate vegetables, nuts and fruits, and drank water. She went into an almost trance-like state in healing herself. She gradually started to come around and delved into hours of motivational speaker videos on YouTube, such as Joyce Meyer, a Christian Preacher whose talks were incredible according to Kim.

They were her life guidance and a glimpse of hope and made it easy to listen on how to deal with bad times. Joyce had the same ideologies as Kim on how the fuck to get through life and that included living life with bravery, and courage, and not playing the victim. Kim had always listened to Joyce Meyer when she felt ungrateful as Kim's desire and desperate obsession to not work also triggered feelings of ungratefulness in her, and she always listened to gratitude talks to stop herself from being a spoilt, ungrateful cow.

Although, Kim wasn't religious and Joyce was Christian, she believed in "IT". She didn't call it God, Allah, Buddha, or whatever the hell the human ego had wanted to brand it. She felt humans shouldn't take whatever the great thing above is and put their idea on what it is, and what it should look like. In her mind, they had almost "branded" the "IT". Branded "IT" with clothes and items such as a cross or a burka.

She cried when she needed to, which was a lot. She tried to stop idealising him. She would float away with dreamy memories of his beautiful, blue eyes looking at her and the way he had been so caring of her once. She remembered it was all fantasy and she knew that people's minds did this when it was craving. They only remembered the good things about people.

So in order to be realistic, whenever your head starts putting that person on a pedestal by having a selective romanticised memory, then try and think of something realistic to counteract the romanticised version. She changed his dreamy eyes to memories of him phlegm-ing up and spitting it on the floor. The times he would take his finger and press it against one nostril and snot onto the floor with the open one.

She remembered the time that she rode him, his eyes were rolling to the back of his head and watering, and it had made her have an orgasm watching him and counteracted it with all the times she had tried to arrange romantic weekends away, only to be continuously disappointed at his erratic, rushed, and stressful ways that made her even more tense than a Monday morning at work had made her.

Her thoughts of his cock going in her slowly and the first time he said "you're mine now" were replaced with thoughts of her after long, stressful days, huge meals and exhaustion, and then having acrobatic sex with no foreplay or build-up. Even though now she would love a good fuck from him. She would have loved that sex from him if only in the afternoon.

Her mind wandered off back to how well the sex could have developed if he had been with her at her peak time in the daytime. But a fat chance. She almost felt angry at herself that he hadn't seen a sexual side to her that wasn't available to him after a day of stress. She felt like she should have done better and started to torture herself once more on re-thinking how she should have handled things, and what if she had done this or that.

She rattled herself back to reality and told herself to stop being a dick head. No woman in her right mind who works all day or has kids all fucking day is going to be some late-night sexual goddess and be so grateful to have her pussy rubbed so hard like it was some sort of winning scratch card. Her mind was 100mph and she had exhausted herself. She would revert back to comments he had said to her and overthink the meaning of them.

She remembered not so long back, that he had said to her, 'Your hair is so soft, it's not like other girls' hair whose are all knotty. I can run my fingers straight through yours; it's beautiful.' She hadn't thought much of the comment at the time but now though, her mind was analysing and dissecting everything like a puzzle. Who was he comparing her hair to? When had he been stroking his manly hands through another woman's hair, giving another woman comfort?

She was angry that he might have shoved his dick in some slag's mouth and not given her the time of day, but to run his fingers through another woman's hair. She was pleased though in some weird way that she had the softest hair and had won that small battle at least.

A few months had passed, and Kim had battled halfway through the pain. Spring was here yet again, and she had become obsessed with cycling as to try and get through the weekends as that's when the mental torture would start. She compared Mushy to heroin because love sets off the same receptors as opioids. It doesn't matter how toxic things are with relationships, chemicals get released from the brain upon cuddling and kissing and endorphins and feel-good chemicals drip from your brain all the way through to your stupid heart.

Now this person becomes your drug. You seek the high but ignore the fact that you're sticking a needle in your arm to get it. Love is blind. But Kim was as strong as an ox. She could beat it she was sure. It hurt that he hadn't reached out to her, but she knew he didn't give a fuck so that helped with the detox. She had cycled subconsciously in a trance to where they had once had one of their first dates.

As she dismounted her bike and sat on the grass, she realised where she was, and she became nervous, this was one of her spiritual moments. She felt him in her presence and it was a sign that she was going to bump into him as she had with every other person that she had experienced this with. Sure enough, as she was about to mount her bike and cycle off quickly time, he appeared with Aggie on the path.

Kim did not know where to put herself and she wanted the ground to swallow her. If he loved her, she would have been angry, and she would have for sure, out of her love for him, scratched his good eye off. But as she knew he had no feelings for her, it was pointless and more embarrassing than anything. She felt embarrassed that she had meant so little to him, embarrassed that he had made a fool out of her, and had lied to her for so long.

They locked eyes and as soon as Aggie found Kim's scent, she came bounding over and knocked Kim down with her sheer loving strength. Kim had been heartbroken to lose her Aggie but what could she do, it was his dog after all. He sheepishly came over to retrieve Aggie. It was all so strange. In Kim's life not so long ago, this was her family. These two beings had become home for her and now they were almost strangers passing each other on a walk.

Kim composed herself and mustered up the words 'I had a feeling I would bump into you here. I promise I am not stalking you, I am just out on a cycle.' She smiled, but she hated having to talk like this, it was all bullshit, all false and not real talk. To her disbelief, Mushy carried on the conversation and it sickened her as she saw in him the same body language and expressions he used when he was talking to Sharlene outside the shops.

It could be deja vu, but only this time, Sharlene was Kim. She had such a sickening realisation then that Kim was just another girl in his long list of victims. He had done this time and time again to women, over and over, replacing one, after the other, after the other. She realised there and then that he was a disposer. He disposed of everything. He collected things, devoured them, and then disposed of them when he was bored.

He wrote down his number and handed it to her sheepishly. It was so bad because Kim knew he didn't even want to give her his number, he just did it out of awkwardness. It was like it was some sort of gift to say sorry. He left and at that point, Kim wished she had the beauty and power to overcome him, seduce him, and then break him into a thousand pieces like he had done to a long line of unsuspecting women.

She wished she had the power to make him suffer, really suffer. But she was nothing really. She couldn't let the thoughts go, though, no matter how hard she tried, all she could think was how could she make herself irresistible again to him so she could fuck him up. From their power struggles, she knew he liked submissive women who would follow him around, stroking his ego, whilst nodding quietly and smiling politely.

Kim knew she was treading in dangerous territory where her mind was concerned. She had done some digging now that she had his number again and discovered from being a master investigator on Facebook that most of his ex-girlfriends were crackheads, single mums, and plain janes.

They didn't have shit on Kim and that is when the hope turned into a fact that if she had been the best of his collection, she could easily dumb herself down, make him obsessed with her again by asking him no questions and being grateful for the crumbs he offered her, making him feel like a big man, stroking his ego, and then the chances of doling out a huge, big shitload of justice pie were in her reach.

She set about obsessively planning in her head. She made sure not to google anything on her phone as she knew the authorities could track your history even if deleted. From her work PC, she googled "household chemicals that can kill humans". The immediate result that came up was the case of a woman who had killed her husband by lacing his steak and kidney pie over a few weeks with weed killer.

Mushy had severe COPD, alcoholism, heart problems, smoked copious amounts of weed and tobacco, and was taking an enormous amount of medication for his mental health and back injury. If he died, they probably would not bother to do an autopsy in order to look for poison as the NHS had become so busy and overrun. They would probably pass it off as natural causes due to his health.

Even if they did do an autopsy and found poison, she was sure he had so many enemies over the years including a long line of hurt women and jealous men.

Kim with her clean record, mundane life, and nice character would surely get past the law.

It was a slow process to try and get him back in her good books. He had not responded on the burner phone Kim had purchased and instead was messaging her on FB messenger which was excruciating for her to say the least. She searched his name again on FB and 6 or more different profiles had come up for him. She knew he always lost his phone and so obviously created new ones.

But she was still shocked as after a year, she thought he was not on social media. He tortured Kim by still not using her phone to contact her. He uploaded videos to his new Facebook account that he thought Kim didn't know about. Stories every day of him working on his body and looking good. It was tormenting her soul even more and she couldn't wait for the day to hurt him back.

Thinking about other women watching him, messaging him. She had no choice but to stay cool. She would have to endure it in order to carry out her plan.

She was studying hard on the weed killer but the one that she needed was called Round Up and it had Paraquat in it, which was only sold in the USA. She was getting angrier by the day having to watch his videos and follow them up by stalking the women who had applied a heart emoji. She snooped through one woman's profile—the woman on every profile picture was a slutty tramp.

The sort of slut that men lost their shit over. Big tits, obtainable and good for a dirty fuck. She wreaked filth. Other girls would not see her as competition but Kim knew this sort of woman was the stuff of man's sex dreams. Mushy only had a majority of male friends, but the recently added friends were all his "sort" of women. Single council estate mums. Kim had built up a picture of his kind of woman.

He was unable to give much, so he sought out women who he thought would be grateful for his breadcrumbs. She could see him now doing his heroic act like he did at the shops with that woman on that day. What he probably didn't realise was that council estate single mums are probably less tolerant of men like him as they are skint, fed up and tired, and wouldn't want to waste their time on a man that wasn't going to be a partner and deal with life together as one.

The words "I got you" and "I will have you for life" would wash over a single mum. Single mums want action and so he had his ideas wrong, and it showed in his long line of what he had deemed as grateful women.

As much as Kim would never blame any other woman or fight over a man, she felt the urge to find this woman and tear her face off. The burning pain of thinking about what he had been up to. Had they talked? Had they met? Does he go and see her in Leeds? Had he been with them both at the same time? She wished she could drop it and move on, but her decision to kill him had already been made and she was gleefully happy about it.

She thought hard mostly at night on how to find the perfect plan, how to not get caught. If she killed him at her house then how would she dispose of the body? She could drive the body somewhere or hide it. Could she put it in the garden, somehow chop him up, and burn him bit by bit on the pit fire? Nothing was feasible. All of her neighbours could see into her garden and there would be witnesses to make statements of him coming to her house.

If she drove him somewhere to dump the body, then her car would be on cameras and her phone would be picked up on the signal posts. You would have to be so clever nowadays to get away with murder. Plus he was 6ft plus and built like a brick shit house, and no match for her.

The only way she could get away with it was at his trailer and with weed killer in his food. But she had no way of getting the correct weed killer and she wasn't even on his radar to be with him. She researched some more and smiled heavily when she came across an article about a poisonous flower called aconite. It was native to North America and Europe, but they had some in blossom in the late summer in Wales and people were being fiercely warned not to touch it.

The plant, if ingested, caused severe respiratory and cardiac problems. It was fucking perfect. The effects of it matched his health conditions and Kim felt the butterflies in her stomach knowing this was meant to be. Apparently, it tasted foul, so she would have to disguise it in a venomously hot curry. It was spring, so Kim had a few months to perfect her moves and then put her plan into action.

Mushy turned up at her house. She melted at the sight of him. It was a relief to feel his hug and his touch again and connect with love. She knew they both loved each other but the opposing magnets were still there in the background. They embraced in the kitchen and started to kiss, and he went full force 0-60, but it felt different. It felt as if he was trying to show her what she had been missing.

His effort was always good but this time, it felt almost sadistic in the way he was trying to make her remember him.

Almost like a goodbye fuck. The next day, her best friend was coming to stay for the weekend and she thought he must have been trying to just impress her as he might have thought that she was going out to the pubs where there would be other men. Almost like a territorial fuck.

Little did he know, Kim and her friend loved nothing more than to sit with a cup of tea and biscuits watching gogglebox and belly laughing over old memories of their past lives working in Magaluf.

It was Saturday and she had a text from him at 16:30 that his mum had been taken into hospital. She texted him on WhatsApp and FB Messenger all night through to Sunday morning but nothing, no reply. She had a reply from his mum to say he was not at the hospital with her, so she knew his mum was ok and assumed he had lost his phone on a bender.

He had promised to take her for dinner on Sunday and when he finally texted at 13:30 with a video message of him walking the dog and no response to any of her previous messages, she was a bit irritated. She wanted to kick off but she had to play it sweet. "Have you not had my messages?" she asked. He replied with a "no". She couldn't hold her cool and replied, "Funny that because no fucker else has ever had a problem receiving my messages but you".

He replied almost immediately with a voice note, "Watch this now, watch, you slavering on again. It's done".

She replied more calmly and said, "Sorry for wanting to see you and worrying, I just love you, babe. I was worried and wanted to see you". He never replied and she deleted his number hoping he would respond sooner or later.

A week had passed and she knew he had deleted all existence of her and blocked her on all communications. She didn't feel worried as she was hopeful it was just a hiccup and he would calm down sooner or later. She re-activated her Facebook to have a nose. She didn't bother looking at his profile as nothing ever came of it, but as she was browsing, his name caught her eye.

She clicked on the person you may know notification with super speed, and it said, "In a relationship with Mushy Mushy". This Sharlene Seers is in a relationship with him. She quickly clicked on him and it was reciprocated by him too. She felt like a knife had gone through her heart. They both had uploaded a profile picture of them kissing and both had put it on public. She could not even catch her breath. She scrolled through this other woman's page.

She was around 50 years old, haggard, frumpy, and low and behold, she was a landlady of a pub. Kim had a weird sigh of relief that like the previous women, she was not a scratch on Kim. She laughed and whispered the words 'Thank fuck,' because if who he had left her for was better than her, then she would not have been able to cope with it. She would have spiralled out of control with self-loathing and would have awful feelings of low self-esteem and worth.

This, in fact, gave her a boast of almighty confidence that she hadn't felt in years. She knew, of course, nothing was about looks but fuck me when you're a woman it helps that your miles better than the trog your man has left you for. In some subconscious way, she also knew that Mushy was an alcoholic, so a woman running a pub 10 minutes away from where he lived with ever-flowing alcohol was a no-brainer for him. She sat trying to take it all in when a burning vile came up her throat.

She realised about his goodbye fuck and the fact that he had been fucking this old hag at the same time as he had been fucking Kim. Sharing a dick with this Peggy Mitchell-looking creature was enough for her stomach to churn to pieces. She couldn't show anyone she knew. She had to stay silent but if he did come back to Kim again, then she knew there was no way in hell she would ever go near his cock ever again.

She would projectile vomit at the thought. So how would she seduce him now? She quickly de-activated Facebook. She knew he would pipe up sooner or later, so she had to sit back and think.

It was June, and she booked a coach ticket using cash payment at Leicester Train Station. July was when the aconite was in bloom and so now was the time to start. The flowers bloomed in Rhayadar in Powys. Over the month, she purchased gloves, eye protection, a facemask, plastic containers, battery backup chargers, bottled water, and a large backpack. She had gone to Birmingham for a day and brought a blonde ombre lace front wig and a black stylish ladies' tracksuit and trainers. She wanted to make sure nobody would recognise her on any CCTV.

At last, after 3 changes, a short walk, a bus journey, and another long walk, she reached The Crown Inn B&B in Wales. She had chosen it as it had a floral ceiling design in the entrance lobby which seemed apt for her stay. She checked in with a usual over-friendly Welsh lady. She loved Welsh people, mainly their accents. Lee was from Wales, and she had always dreamt of one day him getting his act together and taking her away to go and live in Wales with his family.

Even though he was from Llanelli, which was far from glamorous, but it still was close to the Welsh Hills and had a beach that she could walk on every day with the dogs they would have. The lady showed her to her room. It had a shed door and low ceiling with wooden beams, and a red carpet that you would find in an old 70s pub. It reminded her of her upbringing. The Saturdays in the family room at the pub after the food shop.

All the mum's and dad's drinking in the main bar and the children in the family room, all playing together high on panda pops and bags of salt and vinegar chip stick crisps, running in and out to the bar collecting as many 20ps as possible to buy the gobstoppers from the dispense machine. Whenever Kim travelled anywhere, it always brought on deep nostalgic thoughts of her happy childhood. She often wondered if that was why she was so deeply sad as she could not get back the freedom of childhood.

The only decision to be made is whether to play hide and seek or British bulldog. She had grown up with a large gang of boys and there was only her and another girl on the street, and so they were both Tom Boys and both fighters. They were the first to prove themselves, whether it be the first to climb a tree or the first to knock on a door when playing knock door run. Kim often walked around the old street that she grew up in as it was near to where she was living.

The woods near her house still had the ropes she and her friend had tied to the tree to make a tree swing. They were at best 30 years old but the frayed ropes were still there. She ran a boiling hot bath in the deep tub and relieved her aching body from the long journey. Her inner voice was piping up and telling her that life was worth living and that this stupid idea could imprison her, and she would have to spend her life in prison.

Maybe prison would be nice? Maybe she would be happy in prison. It would be like childhood again. People would feed her, and look after her, she would have no bills or work to worry about. She would form deep bonds which she so venomously craved. 'Dick head, you are nuts, Kim,' she whispered to herself. She got into the huge bed, pulled up the thick sheet and felt wonderful.

It was lovely in this room. There was a good aura and she felt that whatever spirits or energy were present in this room, they were smiling down on her and approving of her soul. She drifted off into a deep, secure sleep.

Kim made her way to the bike shop and hired out a bike for the day. She left a £200 deposit as she had persuaded the man to believe her when she had told him she had forgotten her ID. She rode out to the meadows and was stunned at how beautiful it was. Elan Valley, Green mounds, flowing lakes, it was spectacular and not a person in sight. She was very well prepared with her 4 battery backups, and so would have enough battery to navigate on her phone map.

She had her hiking boots on, waterproof leggings, and mac and a foil blanket—even though it was summer, it still could get cold and wet if she got lost and had to spend the night there. The Elan Valley was so vast and she felt like she was in another world. It was so tranquil and she intermittently stopped to gaze at the sun glistening of the water. The only sounds were of the sheep in the near background.

She felt this is what it must feel like to be on heroin and had never understood why people did not seek out this sort of bliss instead of reaching for a needle to stick in their arm. At least this was a real experience. A real utopia that they could all enjoy here on earth, and nobody needed to get hurt in the process. She had directed the sat nav to where the aconite grew and after 4 hours of cycling and stopping to admire things, she arrived in the meadow.

The plant was spectacular. She could only look at it in awe. They were as big as her and she felt butterflies as she knew she was in the process of putting that cunt to bed very soon. There was still nobody in sight and she had not seen one person on her whole journey. She put on her protective gear and opened up the black bag ready to fill. She took the cutters and started from the top, snipping small pieces, and placing them carefully in the black bag.

She especially concentrated on the roots, trying to pull up and chop as much as the root as she could as that was apparently where the poison was more prominent. She sealed the bag with elastic bands and double-bagged it.

The 4-hour journey back to the bike shop felt like it went quickly. She was so happy and exuberated that she was here, putting her plans into action, taking revenge on the cunt who had used her, messed her around and crushed her heart ruthlessly for the last year or so.

She arrived back home, dropped the bag into the kitchen, tidied up and organised herself to prepare for more next steps and plan progression. She cycled up to the local food store and purchased all the ingredients to make a Madras Curry plus some extra spicy food stuffs to disguise the taste and smell if there was one like it had said in her research. She arrived back in the kitchen and her stomach was in knots with excitement.

She set to work on powdering the plant. She again put on her mask, goggles, and protective clothing, removed her cats from the house, and began dropping patiently and slowly bit by bit of the plant into the food processor, watching it grind and powder beautifully. The batch was huge. She needed to ensure he would die and was taking no chances for him to survive. She was ensuring revenge for not just herself but for all of the other previous women he had used and fucked over as well.

The curry was easy to make and she separated some for herself into a plastic container and secured it tightly with a lid and put it out of the way. The remaining batch was laced heavily with all of the powder from the plant and transferred to a big container, secured with a lid and put on the side. She opened all of the windows, cleaned up immaculately the kitchen, and ensured all traces of dust were gone before removing her mask and gear carefully in the garden shed.

She showered and made herself look glowing. She was not able to message him to say she was coming to see him to bring him dinner. It was all fate from now on. Nobody was to know she was to go there that day. As far as everyone was aware, including Mushy, Kim was old news. He was now with his girlfriend/mum, heavily drinking the profits from her pub, and it was clear he was an alcoholic on a very bad scale, which was more than Kim had ever known actually.

She knew he had a drinking problem, but when she looked at his pictures, she had seen the same dead eyes in him as any other addict. He was incredibly ill health looking, which was perfect for the plan. Kim needed more than anything day for fate and demons to be on her side.

She dosed herself one final time in the perfume that he loved and used to spray on his pillow when she was not there. She took the plastic containers and started to drive through the familiar country lanes towards his trailer. Her heart was beating similarly to the first time she had made this journey.

A wave of panic went through her at the prospect of him being at home with somebody else or not in at all.

She pushed the thoughts out of her head and concentrated on fate and the demon's company that sat in her soul, willing her that all would be well and not to even bother thinking that her plan would not work. It was fate. She pulled up in a village around a 30-minute walk from his area.

She had left her phone at home and she had disguised herself in her ombre wig, and a sports cap, and she wore cycling shorts, a tracksuit top, and trainers. With her backpack and bottle of water, she started to jog on the country road leading up to his trailer. Nobody would have batted an eyelid as this was a jogger and cycle path paradise.

She got to the site and it was deathly quiet. She had gone round the back way through a field and a wire fence with a big hole in it, which led straight into the back area of his trailer and not one camera or person could have seen her she was sure of it. It was as silent as she remembered when she had first come here and her heart hurt a little at how in love she was with him and the pain of it not being reciprocated. She looked at the open door and could hear the TV playing the news and she knew he was home.

She knew he would be asleep on his sofa, and it was just how she wanted him. Sleepy and on his tablets. She knew if he was asleep sometimes in the afternoon, his head would have probably been playing up and he would have taken tonnes of sleepers and opium-based painkillers.

She stepped through the door with the dinner containers in her hand. He was, as assumed, asleep. She looked at his beautiful face. He had all the features of a deadly beautiful person, such as a huge square jaw, high cheekbones, olive skin, a beautifully shaped mouth with juicy lips, big bushy but shaped eyebrows, super long and super thick eyelashes, dimples, and a 5 o'clock shadow which added to his beautiful roughness.

She put the containers on the table, got on her knees and stared at his face with close proximity to study his beauty more, almost hypnotised by him. She wished that his beauty could have also reflected in his soul. He opened his eyes suddenly and Kim swerved a punch in the head as he jolted up. As he came back down to reality and realised it was her, he looked at her with discontent and hate that made Kim reeve with uncomfortableness.

'Babe, I know that you don't want me here, I can see from your face that I should not have come here. I am so sorry. Now I realise 100% that you don't want me. I am sorry, it was a mistake to come. Let me just eat this dinner that I made for us, and I will go. I am so sorry.' His eyes welled up with tears a little bit, perhaps it was pity or maybe guilt. Unbeknown to Kim (he thought), he had a new girlfriend and Kim did not know and now was he feeling guilty?

Or did he love her still and have been playing games still? She ignored his small tears and started to tip all of his curry into the saucepan to heat up. As it was heating, she knelt down at his seated level for one last chance to glance into those bright, ice-blue devil-feeling eyes. She took his head into her hands and gently kissed his eyes and forehead, and started to lose herself as his huge hands lifted her to a standing position and continued to grasp his hands on her thighs and tiny waist and started to bite her inside leg edging closer to her pussy.

An image of the dirty old hag he was now in a relationship with came at the forefront of her head and bile immediately crept up into her throat and the urgency to carry out the plan quickly came back to her. 'Babe, let's have this dinner quickly as I am so hungry.' She battled him off of her and served him the curry up with a baton of crusty bread and butter. She started to warm her version up in a different pan stating she had made hers separately due to not liking spice.

He loved his food, mainly because he was constantly stoned and so he loved food, and by the time she had turned around to sit down with hers, he had finished it all.

Kim could see his tablets were kicking in as his eyes were rolling, and he was half falling asleep. She ushered him to come and lie down on the bed and he stumbled, spliff in mouth onto the bed and into her arms. He did not try and be sexual as the tablets were truly in effect and Kim thanked her lucky stars as she couldn't bear the thought of sharing dick, and so if she had rejected him, the plan may not have worked, but fate and the demons were with her all the way.

He pulled her as close as possible like he used to and as he drifted off, he looked at her and said, 'You always escape. You always leave me all alone.' She kissed his forehead and smelled his hair as he drifted into a deep sleep. She did not want to stay around to watch any effects starting to take place. She picked up his phone and car keys with a tea towel and placed them just outside his trailer to make it seem like he had fumbled in his pocket and dropped them on the way in.

This way he could not ring an ambulance or drive anywhere. She knew he would not be able to move anyway but wanted to make sure all aspects were covered. She rinsed out the containers and sprayed air freshener to try and disguise any perfume smell, even though the curry had done a good job. The windows were all open along with the door and so any smells would disappear shortly.

She headed out back through the hole in the fence and jogged back the 30 minutes to her car. God, she needed that jog to clear the adrenaline and shock that she had finally done it. She sat in her car and as she pulled away, she knew this was the end of an era and that she would be never driving up those country lanes again. Life was going to take on a whole new path for her. 'You don't fuck with people's hearts. Karma is a bitch, and my name is Karma.' She smiled to herself.

Daniel Kilroy Filder

28 March 1986-3 July 2022

We are deeply saddened to announce the passing of our dearly beloved friend and family member, Daniel Kilroy Filder. Daniel died this morning of natural causes. It is a great loss for all of us. We will dearly miss his big character and we will remember his spirit with a smile.

The wake will be held at St Mary's Church, 101 Saffron Road, Wigston, LE18 4UT on 20 July 2022 at 14:00.

Light refreshments and a celebration of his life will be held at:

The Railbrew Pub
Church Road
Kibworth Beauchamp